A Big House for Little Men

Michael W. McKay

iUniverse, Inc.
New York Bloomington

This is a work of fiction. All of the characters, names, incidents,
organizations, and dialogue in this novel are either the products of the
author's imagination or are used fictitiously.

iUniverse books may be ordered through booksellers or by contacting:

iUniverse
1663 Liberty Drive
Bloomington, IN 47403
www.iuniverse.com
1-800-Authors (1-800-288-4677)

Because of the dynamic nature of the Internet, any Web addresses or
links contained in this book may have changed since publication and
may no longer be valid. The views expressed in this work are solely those
of the author and do not necessarily reflect the views of the publisher,
and the publisher hereby disclaims any responsibility for them.

ISBN: 978-1-4401-5540-6 (sc)
ISBN: 978-1-4401-5538-3 (hc)
ISBN: 978-1-4401-5539-0 (ebook)

Printed in the United States of America

iUniverse rev. date: 07/14/2009

"Old soldiers never die; they just fade away."

—General MacArthur

"Keep your friends close and your enemies closer."

—Sun-Tzu (400BC) Chinese General
and Military Strategist

Acknowledgments

I would like to offer my thanks and appreciation to my family for their support in writing this book. Oh yes, and Frank, our family pug, who sat by my feet and kept me company the whole time I was writing it.

Special Thanks
Codey and Chase - Fort Collins, Co.
Phil and Linda—the most honest couple I have ever met.

Manny and Family
Anna, Rafael, Manny, Brianna
Bobby Murphy – Thanks for being there. I have not forgotten you my friend!

R.I.P.
Johnny and Sean

Introduction

Cody grew up in an all-Irish Dorchester neighborhood in the city of Boston. He lived in the ghetto and learned about real life at the early age of twelve. Not only was he exposed to the streets and crimes that existed within this city, but he also learned the real meaning of "life on the streets."

Cody wanted one thing, to succeed, and he strived to get there. Most kids in the ghetto had three choices in life: to either to become a priest, a cop, or a criminal. Cody chose the latter of the three because he loved the streets. It was in his blood from running wild at an early age. With no stable family life, he chose to become a part of the street society. He roamed day and night. He hated just about everyone and never trusted a single soul. He hated going to school because they could never teach him what he really wanted to know or what he wanted to become. Only the streets could.

Cody came from a family of eight, and they all fended for themselves. They were poor, and he was the second youngest child, brought up with a father he only met twice a year. His dad gave him spare change from his pockets. That was all Cody remembered of him. Cody loved his mom but was never around her because he feared he would bring more trouble to his family like his brothers did. That morning Cody and his mom argued, and as he walked out he slammed the door and heard his mother ram the deadbolt home behind him. "Don't bother coming home," she screeched, before her voice faded into a Valium haze. Cody flew down the rickety stairway that led to his family's tenement. Once on the street, he breathed deeply and adopted the swagger of his older brother Chad, who died up in the big house while doing time for stabbing a guy in a bar room fight. Cody had walked that way ever since he saw his first murdered corpse, in that very stairway two years ago.

Cody was ten years old. He knew the guy, the neighborhood wino who was happy each day and slept on the streets every night. One morning, Cody came down the stairs to go to school and saw the wino lying in a pool of blood. His throat had been cut from ear to ear, and the knife had been rammed through the deceased's right eye. Cody never forgot what he saw. He stood there for five minutes or so and wondered if the wino would ever get up and why someone would do that to him. He had been a happy guy that had nothing and hadn't harmed anyone. But then Cody realized that was the place he lived and that was how life really was. So he went on to school and never spoke about it to anyone.

Cody had everything he needed all around him. He learned from everybody he associated with, from the tough kids on the street corners to the gangsters who ran a section of Boston. Cody aspired to become a juvenile delinquent and succeeded at an early age and so did the other kids he hung around with. At that point, Cody's future as he knew it was carved out for him, and the people who knew Cody—the cops, prison officials, prison inmates, judges, attorneys, district attorneys, and some politicians that still hold office to this day—would never forget him.

Cody dealt drugs, committed armed robbery, was convicted of second degree murder, and at seventeen years of age, he was sentenced to spend his life behind prison walls. He quickly made a reputation for himself within the prison society. He took over and ran the toughest prison in Massachusetts and, at that time, it was known to be the worst in the country. He escaped twice while serving his life sentence and once even jumped off a thirty-foot prison wall to be free.

The inmates classified as psychopaths and sociopaths learned quickly to stay out of his way because of how he gained his rapid rise to power. He had learned how the prison system operated and took advantage of it. Cody was that quiet young kid that listened to everyone's stories with a calm smile, and he remembered everything about each person he met.

Not only did he grow to power, but he was feared by most of the inmate population that had to abide by his rules in the maximum security hellhole.

Prison was just the beginning of life for Cody, and he adjusted over time. He helped recruit and form young execution squads within the prison system and then went to extreme measures to take full control over all of the drugs, booking, extortions, and corruption.

Learn how this young man beat the system after serving over fifteen years within the correction system. Not only did he walk out of prison with a life sentence over his head, but because of the paths he crossed and the power he obtained, his life parole was eliminated like it never existed. In prison, he and his friends had been charged with several murders and running executions squads while serving their time. Cody never was convicted of any of those murders. He did, however, receive more time added on to his original life sentence after his two prison escapes. But somehow, his original sentence was erased. Now he is free and living somewhere in this country.

He is just your average man. He comes and goes as he pleases, free to roam and do whatever he wants, despite being exposed and involved within the worst kind of corruption at the highest level. This story has never been revealed until today. Find out how it all happened. Find out what went through Cody's mind and see how he looks back on his life thirty-five years later. Is he one of your neighbors? A co-worker? An ordinary church-going family man? Or is he just your everyday, run-of-the-mill nice guy who will let you pass in front of his car, give you a friendly nod with a smile on his face, and then run you the fuck over?

Is he real? Could someone make up such a fetishist story

about such a person, and if so, what does this person do in the future with all that hate he could never get rid of? You will be shocked as you live Cody's life, from the streets to prison and back to the streets again.

Chapter One

Back in the day, Boston was known as the city of corruption and the birthplace of gangsters. Some of the very best gangsters came out of Boston, from the famous names of mobsters who ran South Boston (Southie) and had most of the authorities in their pockets, to the other Irish guys called the Winter Hill Gang who ran Somerville and Cambridge, and then over to the North End with the Italians running the north side of town.

It was never a secret who ran what and which section. It was all about who you knew and what you had on that person. All of the tough guys and big gangsters always had something on someone or someone in their pocket, but 95 percent of all gangsters where rats (informants). They would give up somebody or feed something to the cops or the Feds just to keep everyone happy and just to have that favor owed to them in the future. But if someone informed on any of them, they would have had that person killed and his or body would have been dumped into the Charles River.

Cody used to watch these guys very closely. He studied their actions and how they worked. They were smart in a lot of ways. They had nothing to do each day except plan shit and think of how to get away with it. They used everybody and everything they could to gain control and power. Cody thought it was great and so easy to do because everybody wanted fast money. They set up scores and sent people out to steal for them and bring the items back, and then they would pay the people shit. They took no risk. They were like the pimps and everyone else were their whores.

Cody used to laugh every time the cops showed up for their money, but then he thought about the times those same cops arrested people he knew. That was when he understood how all of those guys worked. The gangsters watched the kids in their own backyards (the neighborhoods they ran). Any kid who was trouble, they wanted to recruit. To Cody's luck, he was the most wanted kid around by the gangsters from an early age.

Cody stole anything he could put in his pocket, carry off, or drive away with and sell. The gangsters had one rule: Never play in your own backyard. If you pulled any crime, it had to be out of the neighborhood you lived in. Cody had his own friends from when he was arrested and placed in Department of Youth Services (DYS) and from meeting other kids from Charlestown (the townies), Mission Hill, Hyde Park, and Southie. He grew young with Johnny, his partner. They were like brothers. Nothing kept them apart.

Cody and Johnny knew a lot of kids over in Southie who got tattoos—a dot between their thumb and index fingers—that represented a large gang over there call the Saints. Cody and Johnny were offered the chance to join but turned it down because they didn't want to be used by the gangsters or told what to do. The gangs over there exist to this day, and they are followed by other generations of families.

Cody and his young associates never respected gangsters and mob figures. Those kids didn't give two shits about any of those guys. But at the same time, everyone knew they had to accept the way life is and not get killed by those bastards. So when Cody stole cars and striped them down, he went to Roxbury to sell the parts, for cheap money. Most people in the ghetto paid using their welfare checks and liked driving fine cars. He was taught how to hate and grew up never trusting anyone from a different race, like all his friends did. However, when it came to making money race wasn't a factor. He sold all his stolen items around Boston just to establish and set up his own connections. Cody and his friends would then drive out to the Boston suburbs and break into houses and fence the shit to the gangsters just to keep them happy.

Cody went to the DYS many times as a juvenile. It was like a second home to him. He never minded it. It was like a meeting house for him and all of his friends to gather and get a break from the streets. They got three meals a day and a bed, and they were released within one to three months. It was like a vacation, and the best part was that each time Cody got released; he had the same probation officer, Dave. They became very good friends. Cody found out Dave had a cocaine habit and started supplying to him. They formed a close relationship and stayed that way for a long time.

One day, Cody had to go to Dorchester Court from the DYS for stolen car charges, and they—the DYS—did not want to transport him or his partner Johnny. Johnny was a runner, and when he ran, people had a hard time catching him. So they sent two state troopers to get both of them. Troopers Chase and Callahan showed up and took them both outside. Chase opened his trunk, took Johnny, and put him in the fucking trunk.

"You're not running on me you little fucker!" he told Johnny.

He then put Cody in the back seat of the car. Johnny was pissed all the way to the courthouse because he had been planning to run that day and being free. It was a good laugh for years to come.

Everyone knew Trooper Mark Chase had been a rookie cop back in the '70s. He grew up in Dorchester, but people on the streets knew he was fair and that he never forgot where he came from. Cody had come to know Trooper Chase one night when he was working the Mass Pike with three other kids. Trooper Chase pulled their car over.

After pulling each of them out of the car and starting his search, Trooper Chase found a starter pistol on Cody and about eighteen keys on his key ring. He could not figure out why Cody had so many keys, but Cody knew the keys belonged to stores throughout the inner city of Boston. He had friends that worked in the stores, and they made copies of keys to the front or back doors so Cody and his friends could just unlock the door, take anything they wanted, and lockup when they were done.

Trooper Chase refused to give Cody back his starter pistol, which only fired blanks. Anyone could buy those pistols at a lot of stores in Boston for fewer than twenty bucks, and they looked like real guns. Cody used the pistol just for show and because he knew he never could be arrested for having it.

"If you want this, pick it up at the state police barracks," Trooper Chase told Cody. He then tossed Cody the keys and told them to move on and to have a great night.

Cody was happy about getting the keys back, but he was pissed off that Trooper Chase took his starter pistol. After he pondered it over for a few hours, Cody woke his partner Johnny up around 2:00 AM and asked him for a ride up to the police barracks to get his pistol back. His other friends started laughing and thought Cody was crazy. They told him to go buy another one in the morning.

Cody looked at them and yelled, "Trooper Chase had no right to take it." It was the principle of the matter, and he wanted it back right then.

"Okay, let's get this out of your system so I can get some sleep tonight," Johnny yelled back.

Later, while driving up to the barracks, Johnny said to Cody, "Sometimes I don't understood how you think. Do you really think these cops are going to give you back your starter pistol?"

When they arrived at the police barracks, Cody walked in and saw a big fucking trooper sitting behind the desk. Cody approached the desk, as boldly as could be.

"Are you in charge here?" he shouted. He looked at the trooper's name tag, which read "Sgt Stone."

Before Sergeant Stone could say anything, Cody demanded the starter pistol Trooper Chase had taken from him. Sergeant Stone couldn't believe that Cody, a five-foot-nothing kid weighing

130 lbs, had the balls to walk into a state police barracks and demand anything. The sergeant flew over the counter, grabbed Cody, picked him up with one hand, and threw him face-first into the front doors. He then took Cody outside, asked him if he was playing with a full deck, and told the boys to get a move on or they would regret it.

Cody jumped into the car and slammed the door shut, cursing with every word he knew.

Johnny smiled and looked over at him. "How did you make out partner? Did you get what you came here for?"

"Just drive," Cody said, "and don't say a fucking word to me."

Johnny laughed hard. "Your feet weren't even touching the ground when that trooper was carrying you through those doors." He got Cody to smile.

"Yea, he was a big bastard," Cody said. "When he jumped over the counter at me, I thought he was going to kick my ass."

That incident gave the troopers something to remember as their first encounter with Cody. A few weeks later, Cody saw Trooper Mark Chase parked in his police car outside a hot dog stand up in Mattapan. The fucker was rolling a joint in his cruiser, with a beer between his legs. Cody snuck up on him and banged on the cruiser door

"Hey Trooper Chase," he said, scarring the shit out of the guy.

Trooper Chase jumped and the pot flew everywhere. He rolled down the window of his car and yelled, "What the fuck, Cody? That was my last joint."

Cody just laughed. "Relax. Here's some more." He threw him a dime bag.

Trooper Chase laughed, shook his head, and started rolling again. "You had a lot of balls to try to get your starter pistol back," he told Cody. "You were the talk of that barracks."

They smoked a couple of joints and laughed and talked about shit. Trooper Chase was about nine years older than Cody. They had grown up in the same neighborhood, and he knew Cody's family. Little did each of them know at the time, they would meet again twenty years later and form a bond that is still intact to this day.

Over the past couple of years, Cody had been doing all kinds of small shit—stealing cars, dealing drugs, robbing stores, and breaking into houses—but it somehow was not enough for him. It was like he was on a high and wanted to get higher, but at the same time it was all fun and games for Cody and his friends.

Sometimes they would grab a stolen car just for fun, remove its brake lights, and look for a cop on a motorcycle. They would get the motorcycle cop to chase their car, and just when the cop got close enough, Cody would hit the brakes. The cop would fly over the car or wipe out, and Cody and his partners would take off laughing. That was the mind-set of Cody and his friends.

Chapter Two

One day, Cody received a phone call from his probation officer, Dave. Cody asked him what he needed. Dave was in a panic. He told Cody he needed to meet with him right away. Cody thought he just needed some cocaine.

They met in downtown Boston near the train station. Dave asked Cody if he could get a hold of a couple of guns and if he would mind riding up to New York to help him take care of a personal matter. Cody took a step back and wondered what the hell was up. It was quiet for a moment.

"You know I can get guns," Cody told Dave. "But why do you want to take me on a six-hour drive to New York?"

Dave explained to Cody that his sister had been missing for the past three months. A friend of his informed him she was up in New York and some bonehead kept her on drugs and pimped her out up there in the city. He wanted to find the fucker and bring his sister home.

Cody knew that they were getting close and that Dave let him do anything he wanted, but Dave's request blew Cody's mind. Dave promised he would cover everything up if there was a problem or if something happened. "If this fucking pimp bastard has to get shot, then so be it."

What the hell? Why not? Cody figured. No matter what happened, it could only work out for him down the road.

So they drove over to where Cody hid his weapons and Cody grabbed a .22 eight-shot pistol and his favorite gun, a double barrel sawed-off shotgun, that he carried inside a hammer holster. Nobody could see it under his long black coat in the wintertime.

Cody was always told if he shot someone, he should use a .22 or a shotgun. A .22 would bounce off the bones inside a person's body and would leave no mess, while a shotgun would drop a person quick and leave a big mess. Cody lived by what he learned on the streets, and when he carried a gun, he carried those two so he could chose the gun to fit whatever situation he was in at the time.

Cody had always liked guns. He not only liked the power they gave him, but at fifteen years of age, he couldn't wait to kill a motherfucker and watch him die. He had so much hate built up inside him. He knew it was only a matter of time before he shot or killed someone.

Sitting beside Dave on a six-hour trip to New York, he hoped to unload some of his anger and get the feeling out of his system. As they drove, Dave explained his plan. They had to get his sister out of room 714 in a Manhattan hotel. He wanted to shoot the pimp if he became a problem. Cody told Dave it would be no problem at all and then joked that if they got caught, it wouldn't look good on Dave's resume.

When they arrived in New York, it was snowing and was cold as a mother. Dave pulled up outside the Manhattan hotel. Cody's job was to go into the hotel and tell the guy at the desk his dad was up in the office and he was supposed to meet him. Fooled by Cody's baby face, the guy walked Cody over to the elevators and told him go up to tenth floor.

Cody stepped into the elevator and pushed the button for the tenth floor, knowing he had to get off on the seventh floor and find room 714. He rode up to the tenth just in case the guy was watching the light buttons from the lobby floor. When he reached the tenth floor, he hit the button down to the seventh. Once on the seventh floor, he started to look for lucky room number 714.

He soon found the room and stood outside the door. His heart began to beat faster. He tried to look into the door's peep hole, but he couldn't see anyone moving around inside. He decided to just shoot the fucking pimp when he answered the door and grab the girl if she was in there and bring her down to Dave. In Cody's mind, he had been brought there to kill that son of a bitch, and he liked the idea because someone with authority had given him permission.

So, he aimed his shotgun at the doorknob level, knocked on the door hard, and waited for it to open. No sound came from within the room. He knocked again, and then again. Soon he realized nobody was in the room. Cody returned to the car and informed Dave that neither his sister nor the pimp was there. They decided to wait outside in the car for them to appear. They waited for hours, hoping to see his sister, but she never showed up at the hotel. Discouraged, they drove around to a few bars and had a few drinks. Dave then decided to drive around and ask people on the street if they knew where the pimp named Mule hung out. Each pimp had his own territory, but there were many pimps in New York back then.

Dave and Cody knew they were chasing a dead end. New York was too big for just the two of them, so Dave called it off. He' had the one and only lead to find his sister and realized that today wouldn't be the day they brought her home. They headed back home to Massachusetts.

On the drive back, they talked. Dave wanted his sister back badly, but they both knew it was like looking for a needle in a haystack. But one thing had happened that day. Cody now knew Dave belonged to him. He owed Cody big time for the favor. Cody knew that whatever he needed from Dave from that point on, Dave would be there for him

Why did this guy come to me? Cody thought. *He must have seen something in me other than trust.* Dave had to have known Cody would have no problem at all shooting someone.

A couple of weeks later, Dave found out his sister was found dead in New York from a drug overdose. He and Cody never spoke about it again.

Chapter Three

Cody's older brother Timmy lived in Minnesota and asked Cody if he would come up for a visit. Cody thought about it. *What the hell? Why not?* He figured. It would keep him out of trouble for a while and be like a vacation. He packed one bag of clothes and one gun and took a very long bus ride up to Minnesota. It took about three day to get there.

His brother ran an apartment complex with thirty rooms. He and his wife lived there for free and got paid for it. Timmy had done his shit back in Boston when he was younger, but he had been smart and moved up north to try and get a fresh start. And it had worked out well for him. He had gotten married and had a few kids.

When Cody arrived in Minnesota, Timmy put him up in his own room. He told Cody he could stay as long as he wanted and that he would pay Cody for helping out around the complex. Cody knew his older brother was trying to get him away from the shit back in Boston, but that was not for Cody. After running around in the area, Cody started to meet new people. Before long, he hooked up with others in his own element.

He soon met Emmit. Emmit was a funny bastard. He had been born and raised in the hills of Oklahoma, and he liked the fast life. He and Cody got along fine and started hanging together. They had a lot in common. They both loved to steal cars and make money the fast way. Emmit told Cody he knew a way to make some fast money and have a little fun at the same time. If they drove stolen cars from Minnesota and took them down to Oklahoma, they could get paid by his uncle and then ride back up to Minnesota with another car and get paid again by guys up there.

Cody could not say no to that. Hell, he would have done it just for fun, but money was always nice. They started with one car—a nice, hooked-up 1968 GTO—and took turns driving. It took them about two days to get to Oklahoma. After they received the money for the car, they hung at Emmit's cousin's house for a few days.

Cody had one big problem in Oklahoma. No one in the state sold hard liquor in the 1970s. The supermarket was allowed to sell only beer, and Cody had never heard of the brand. People in the town had plenty of pot, hash, and any drug he could think of, but no whiskey, rum, or gin—nothing. Cody needed his drinks and couldn't wait to get the hell out of there. He would never return to Oklahoma for all the money in the world.

Emmit's uncle told Cody if he wanted the hard stuff he would have to ride up into the woods to get moonshine. It was a drive up into the hills.

"I'm a city boy," Cody told Emmit, "and I'm not going up there in hillbilly country to get hog-tied and fucked by these hicks." They all laughed.

Emmit grabbed another car, and they drove out of that backward state the next day. Little did Cody know that Emmit's uncle was being staked out by the Feds. They followed Cody and Emmit's stolen car all the way back to Minnesota to see where they were taking it. Once they arrived back in Minnesota, the Feds busted everyone and charged them all with transportation of a stolen car across state lines, which was a federal offense.

As luck would have it, Cody was only fifteen and still a juvenile. He used his one phone call to call his friend Dave, his old probation officer. Of course, Dave hooked him up and had an arrest warrant issued for Cody for violation of his probation. That made the Feds release Cody to the warrant. The Feds didn't care about a fifteen-year-old kid. They had their big bust from Minnesota back to Oklahoma.

Dave arranged for Cody to be transported back to Massachusetts. It was great. Cody got locked up for one week in a Minnesota detention center, and then the state of Massachusetts paid for a first-class plane ticket for Cody to return. He got to eat and drink on the plane, and when it landed, the stewardess requested he stay seated on the plane until everyone got off. Then six of Massachusetts' finest state troopers escorted him through Logan Airport like he was a fucking mass murderer.

His buddy Dave was waiting for him near the outside gate. He handcuffed Cody to make things look good and placed him in his car. As they drove away from the airport, Cody slipped the cuffs off. "Here you go, Dave. Thanks for getting me out of this one."

"Anytime," Dave said. He told Cody he'd get that warrant dropped later that day.

He drove Cody to Park Street Station in Boston and handed him two hundred dollars. "Keep in touch."

How great was that? Cody thought to himself. *This is real power. This is how you play the game.* He loved it in a big way.

It felt good to be back in Boston. Cody made a promise to himself that he would never leave Massachusetts again. It was his playground and his home. He now had a better sense of everything around him and felt a lot stronger. From then on, he started to obtain his own people for his own needs and to make a small name for himself among the people he knew.

Chapter Four

He soon hooked back up with Johnny and told him what happened up north. They went back into one of the old neighborhoods where they often hung out, and they ran into one of the head guys from Southie who knew Cody was playing and dealing over in the Mission Hill area. He used to sell some of his stolen treasures there.

Cody and Johnny hung out at a bar called Toni's Place. It was where all of the old ex-cons from prison hung out and did their business. Each and every one of them was always looking to make a buck or two and planning to make a score somewhere.

Toni's Place was a front for a bookie joint for the North End wise guys and was located in a very tough all-minority section of Jamaica Plain (Mission Hill). But the place made money, and nobody fucked with anyone who hung out there. One time, Cody heard three boneheads walked into the bar and tried to rob it, but they hadn't known the kind of guys that hung in there. They were overpowered and turned up missing. Nobody gave a fuck about their disappearance, but nobody ever tried to rob Toni's again.

One of the head guys from Southie owned a small place right across the street from the bookie joint. Nobody ever asked why, but Cody assumed they saw money for their future in that part of town, or maybe they wanted to push the North End guys out on their own time.

It was a very small place and a dive, but they opened a small sandwich shop and asked Cody to run it with one of their guys. They instructed Cody to introduce another guy named Bobby to everyone over at Toni's so people would get to know him. The Southie guys knew Cody could get Bobby on the inside without drawing attention toward their group.

Cody had no idea what they had in mind, but he knew if the guys over at Toni's Place found out who Bobby worked for, they would both end up dead. Cody was never supposed to tell anyone who owned the little sub shop, and it didn't matter if the place made money or not. They were just supposed to sell subs and soda and not deal or fuck around or bring any heat on the place.

The best part about the whole deal was that it had a small room upstairs where Cody could crash for free and make money at the same time by running the small shop from eleven to four each day. Plus it got him closer to the people in the bookie joint across the street. They came over each day to eat and bullshit.

Cody still had his partner Johnny, as well as the friends they had both met over time. They got out a couple of times a week and stole what they could and sold drugs. The money was always there, but Cody and Johnny were never in it for the money. It was all for pleasure.

Johnny ended up meeting a kid named Danny through some friends, and Danny started to get close with Johnny and Cody. Before they knew it, the three were inseparable. Danny was a cool kid. He came from a rich suburb section over in a small town north of Boston. It was a small town, but it was growing into a fast and upcoming city. Danny introduced Cody and Johnny to a well-known thief named Jimmy. He talked about how his hometown was a gold mine for whatever they wanted. It turned out he was right. Jimmy hooked Cody and his two partners up with some of the town's smaller thieves.

Cody started dealing with most of them because he had the cash and drugs and bought everything anyone brought him. It opened up a lot of different avenues for Cody and his partners, all at the age of sixteen, and they recruited a small group of kids to work for them. These suburban guys were nothing compared to Cody and his partners. They broke into a house and took this or that and ran off thinking they hit the big score. Cody would have Danny and Johnny back a truck up to a house like they were moving the people out and take everything, even their pets.

Cody was sixteen now and growing stronger within the town. He was amazed that most of the thieves never wanted cash. They wanted drugs—pills, pot, or heroin. Cody, Johnny, and Danny laughed about how fucked up it was. They all stole that shit to get high for a few hours, and then they would come back with more.

Cody and Johnny were never big on doing drugs. They smoked pot a little and drank their share, but Cody always liked to deal with a clear head. He watched the guys shoot up heroin, then start throwing up every three minutes, and then sit back looking like they had just died. He could never understand it and hated being around obnoxious people, whether they were drunks, dope heads, or just stupid people. Everybody knew one thing about Cody and Johnny: if you're going to be high around either of them it would be fine, but if you were obnoxious and stupid, you would get hit in the fucking head with a bat.

Things were going great for Cody and his partners in the small town on the outskirts of Boston, so one day he took a ride back into Southie with Johnny and told the head guy he couldn't work in that shop over in Mission Hill anymore. He quickly spoke up and told them what he had going on up in the small town.

The Southie guy sat back and smiled. He said he didn't appreciate Cody bailing out on the shop because he had his own reasons, but he agreed to go along with it because he was a greedy fuck. He knew Cody would somehow keep money coming their way and open other avenues to spread out even more. They decided to help Cody and his partners out and arranged for a truck to pick everything up once a week or whenever Cody or his partners called. All of the payments would be paid half in cash and half in drugs. They let one of Cody's friends run the shop over in Mission Hill but insisted Cody stop in once in a while to make an appearance over in Toni's Place and bring them a gift now and then. Cody agreed.

He moved into his little gold mine north of Boston. He loved it there. He was only twenty-five miles from the inner city, but because he was originally from the ghettoes, moving there was like a breath of fresh air. Within six months, he had a nice place and a girlfriend. He had all of the kids around stealing whatever and bringing it to him. All he had to do was make a call over to Southie and they would pick the shit up and pay him and Johnny.

Cody didn't mind dumping the shit off for fast cash and drugs. It kept their connections open, and sometimes they would send people up from Southie or Dorchester for a show of force. It showed everyone who dealt with Cody and Johnny that they had people to back them. In a small town like that, nobody wanted that kind of trouble.

Cody had been pulling crimes in this small town for over a year, and at age seventeen, things were rapidly developing for him and Johnny. The cops were pissed that the crime in their town was getting way out of hand. The town cops were very slow compared to Boston cops. The local town cops in the small suburb towns always had to count on the state police for help with problems.

At that time, the local police still were not on to Cody and his partners. Everything went smoothly until one Sunday morning when two Southie guys Cody knew, Pat and Eddie, came up from Boston. They broke into a furniture store on a main street and proceeded to lug half of the store onto a truck. A town cop was on his way to church and noticed them moving stuff out the back door of the store. He called it in, and the department sent every cop in the area that morning to surround the store.

Pat and Eddie barricaded themselves inside the building and refused to come out. Cody heard the state police sent in a K-9 dog to try to get them out. The dog ran toward Pat, but Eddie grabbed it by the neck. All anyone could hear was the dog barking and then a yelp. Eddie snapped its neck. They then grabbed the ninety-pound German shepherd by its paws and threw it through the front window of the store. At that point, the cops were thinking, *what the hell do we have here?*

Eddie was stoned out of his mind. He jumped up in the window of the store and yelled, "Got any more puppies you want to send in here?"

A loud bang sounded. The K-9 cop shot him right below his nuts and almost took his balls off. Pat just gave up after that, and they both went off to the big house to do ten to twelve years. That was what the cops were looking for—someone to blame for the rising crime in their small towns. Headlines in the local papers read that the police caught gangsters from South Boston robbing their businesses and how Boston was sending the mob up to their communities.

The town officials were smart to make claims like that because it brought more money in from the state and more resources. They brought in more law enforcement and started messing Cody's business up.

The guys coming up from Southie and Dorchester had been pulling crimes at a larger level for months. For a while, Cody and Johnny had no idea they were even in town with them. When he found out, Cody was pissed off about what the Southie guys were doing. He knew who was behind it all, but he knew he couldn't do a damn thing about it. The gangsters were using him and Johnny as front guys again, and now they were trying to come into town and take everything right out from under them.

Chapter Five

Nobody Cody and Johnny knew cared about getting caught or doing time. It was the way of life on the streets. When they were under seventeen, they would usually go to DYS and be out in no time. While they were in DYS, they met more people and got new ideas. But if they were seventeen and older, they went to the state prison, and everyone knew if someone went there, they would be gone for a long time.

The townies back in those days were all Irish guys who robbed banks. That was what they were known for over in Charlestown. Judges threw the book at them and gave them telephone numbers in prison for twenty to thirty years. The system was a little messed up back in those days because people got sentenced big time for robbing a bank, but if someone raped a kid or a woman, they were put in a nut house and let back out onto the streets in six months. Rape was not a crime according to the judges. The system said rapists and molesters were sick and needed help. It was like saying, "Take my wife and kids but not my money."

Cody was involved with one girl he liked very much. It was during that time that Cody's biggest problems began. He became too attached to her. She was an Italian girl named Maria. He was not a guy that liked many people, and he didn't let many people get close to him. Cody knew his new feelings for Maria would only cause him more problems down the road. It was easier to for him to hate people because there were no attachments, but once he started loving or liking someone, things got very complicated.

By that point, Cody had done a lot of shit over the past

five years. He was fine until he got close with Maria. He started feeling obligated to look after her and considered her family his own. They treated him well and welcomed him with open arms, of course with the exception of her asshole father—a big man about six two and weighing in at about 230 lbs. He was a drunk who use to beat his wife and kids all the time when he lived with them. But after his separation from Maria's mother, he just visited time to time.

One Thursday night, Cody was partying with Maria at her house when her drunken ass father showed up. Nobody understood why he showed up that night. He usually came on weekends, never on weekdays. He walked through the door, looked at Cody, and yelled, "Hey, you little shit, are you fucking my daughter?"

Cody didn't respond or even look at him. He just smiled at Maria. "Maybe we should go over to my place," he said.

"Let's hope he will fall asleep soon and sleep it off, or maybe he will leave soon," Maria said.

"I'd hate to drop him where he stands," Cody told Maria.

Maria turned toward him and smiled nervously. "What do you mean by that?" she asked.

Before Cody could answer, Maria's mom stepped in front of her husband and told him to calm down. She threatened she'd call the cops if he started any trouble. The old man sat down and got very quiet and started drinking more and more. Cody knew he should leave right there and then, but he had to stay because he wanted the obnoxious drunk to say one more fucking word to him. Sure enough, after drinking for another half hour, Maria's father started in again. Once again, his wife got up and started yelling at him to stop.

"Shut your mouth, bitch." He stood up and pushed her against the wall, knocking her to the floor. Then he started to turn toward Cody.

Cody drew his pistol and aimed it at him. "Sit the fuck down or I will fucking drop you where you stand."

The old man sat back in his chair, looking at the barrel of the gun. His wife rose to her feet and ran upstairs.

"Cody, please don't do this," Maria said. "Let's leave," she pleaded.

Her father drank another mouthful of whiskey straight from the bottle. "Go head shoot me," he shouted. "You don't have the fucking balls, you fucking faggot."

That was all Cody needed to hear that night. He'd fucking had it with everything and everyone. It was time to do what he had always wanted to do. He wanted to make this fucking obnoxious drunk pay for the poor wino he'd seen with his throat cut when he was ten, for growing up poor, for everyone he hated in life, and for being born into the fucking world.

Cody looked down at the end of the barrel of the gun, aiming at the old man's big-framed body. He cocked the gun once and pulled the trigger. *Bang.* The old man's body jumped. Cody cocked the gun once more. *Bang.* The old man jumped again. It all happened in slow motion and the fucker just sat there, looking at Cody in disbelief. The old man didn't move or say anything at all. For a moment, Cody thought he must have missed, but how could he have missed being that close? He took a step to the right and aimed the pistol at the man's temple. *Bang.* When the bullet hit the old man's head, both of his arms flew up above his head, and then his head and arms bounced against the top of the kitchen table a couple times.

It only took about seven seconds to do, but it seemed like five fucking minutes. For those few seconds, all time was lost and it got very quiet inside Cody's head, except for a loud ringing in his ears from the gun going off. Then he heard Maria yelling and felt her shaking his shoulder. Cody turned and looked into her eyes.

"You're fucking crazy," she shouted and started crying. She ran upstairs yelling, "He just shot dad! He just shot dad! Call the police!"

Cody shook it off and knew he had to get the fuck out of there very quickly. He didn't have a car at her house, so he had to run as fast he could. While running, he heard police sirens coming from every direction. He ran about a half mile over to Joey's apartment and told him he needed his car because he just shot someone.

"What did you do?" Joey asked.

"Don't ask any fucking questions," Cody said.

Joey tossed him the car keys and Cody got in the car and drove out town, heading for Boston. It was the only place he knew where he could get some help and advice.

His mind was numb as he drove. He still had the fucking pistol in his pants. He knew he'd just killed that motherfucker and that he had to go somewhere, but he had no idea where to go. Hell, he didn't even have time to get in touch with Danny or Johnny or have time to look for them.

His mind raced. *Why did I kill that fucking guy?* He thought to himself. There were a lot of other people he would have much rather killed than Maria's father. He knew he had to get control of himself and his thoughts after what had just happened.

He had to get somewhere so he could think and get in touch with his partners. They would help him out. The cops would know who they were looking for, and if they caught him, he would go down for life. *That fucking drunk,* Cody thought. *Why did he come over tonight? Why did he say to go ahead shoot him? Why did he say I didn't have the fucking balls and call me a faggot? What an asshole. Fuck him. He needed to die.*

As Cody drove down the interstate, he saw four state trooper cars sitting on the side of Massachusetts turnpike. When Cody passed them, they pulled out and started to follow him. He wondered how the fuck they knew he was in that car. *That fucking Joey.* Cody figured he must be covering his ass because Cody took his car. Joey probably told the cops on him just in case he would get stopped in his car.

"Son of a bitch," Cody yelled. He had broken his own rule: never trust anybody but himself.

The four troopers stayed about half a mile behind Cody's car, and he began to think they might not be following him. Maybe they were on patrol or going somewhere else. Maybe they were not out for him. Then he thought, *yeah right.*

Cody turned off on the Boston exit and looked in his rearview mirror. The troopers were still tailing him, so Cody figured he would head for the ghettoes and hide deep within the projects. Cody knew the cops hated going into that part of town. The first light he came to off the exit ramp was red. When he went to run it, two Boston cops pulled out in front of his car, blocking off the intersection. It looked like New York's Times Square on New Year's Eve. Suddenly, Cody was surrounded by Boston and state cops. Lights flashed, and the cops had their guns aimed at him.

"Shit!" Cody shouted. He had forgotten to get rid of the gun, another rule he had broken: always get rid of the fucking weapon.

It was decision time. Should he cash in his chips there or let them take him? There was one thing he knew about cops: they let you decide your own fate. They at least gave you that choice.

But he also knew that out of all of the cops pointing their guns at him, one of them would love to go home to his family and say, "Honey I had to kill a bad guy tonight."

Fuck that, Cody thought to himself. He was not ready to die that night, so he put up his hands let them pull him out of the car. They found the gun tucked in the waistband of his pants. From there, they took him up to the state police barracks to charge and interrogate him.

At the barracks, the cops asked Cody a lot of questions. All Cody would tell them was that he had acted in self-defense. He had felt threatened by the big drunk guy and had to shoot him.

One cop leaned over toward Cody. "If you had shot him once and run out of the house and called us, we would have bought that story, but you shot him twice and then moved over and shot him right in the head. We got a problem with that."

"Sounds cold-blooded to me," the other cop yelled.

"Fuck off," Cody said to both of them. "If you don't believe me, then what can I say?"

"We don't need anything from you," the first trooper said. "We got statements from the witnesses and the gun you shot this guy with. You're not getting off. You are going down for life."

Cody had nothing else to say. They escorted him out of the interrogation room and put him into a jail cell. He knew they would charge him with first degree murder. And as he sat in the cell, who should walk up to the bars but the big fucking state trooper Sergeant Stone.

"You know, you little shit," he said, "I should have given you that starter pistol back that night. You couldn't kill anyone with that."

Cody just shook his head. The last time he'd come there, that fucking sergeant had no sense of humor and used Cody's face to push the front doors open. And now, that night of all nights, he wanted to be a fucking comedian.

Chapter Six

Cody was escorted into court the very next morning, which was Friday. The judge charged him with murder in the first degree and sent him over to a prison state hospital for a weekend evaluation to make sure he was competent to stand trial. He arrived at the nut house at around 4:00 PM. After walking through all of the gates, the hospital staff stripped him naked and brought him before three doctors, who were dressed in nice suits and sitting behind a table. He stood there, completely naked, as the doctors asked him questions like, "Do you know what you are here for?" and "Do you take drugs or drink?" After about three minutes or so they nodded to one of the guards, and Cody was escorted naked up to the twenty-room hospital ward.

"Welcome to your home for the weekend," the guard said to Cody and handed him a paper gown to wear and a little bucket.

"What's this bucket for?" Cody asked.

"That's to shit and piss in," the guard said, smiling.

Cody looked into the room, which contained only a mattress on the floor.

"You got to be kidding me," Cody said to the guard. "I'm not fucking suicidal."

"Look," the guard told him. "This is the nut house. Be calm over the weekend till you go to court on Monday, and you better hope you don't have to come back here for further evaluation for another thirty days. If you act up, they will come, tie you down with towels, and shoot you up with some fucked-up drugs that will turn you into a zombie. That's what they do here."

What the fuck kind of place is this? Cody thought to himself.

He stepped into the room, and the guard locked the door behind him. He heard a crazy noise and peered out the door's small window, looking down the hall to see where the weird sound was coming from. Someone was making crazy sounds, but he couldn't see anything.

He sat down on the mattress and looked at the four walls in the dimly lit room, thinking about the past couple of days and how it had taken less than seven seconds to put him in the situation he was in now. There he was seventeen years old, looking at spending the rest of his life in prison. But first, he knew he had to get out of the fucking nut house on Monday morning when he returned to court.

Suddenly, he heard a loud *bang* and then again another *bang*. He ran over to the door and observed several guards with towels standing outside the door where the noise seemed to be coming from. They swung the door open, and a huge black guy came running out to attack them. They forced him to the floor and held him down with towels as a nurse ran over and injected the guy with something. The guy immediately passed out.

What the hell is going on here? Cody wondered. It got very quiet after that, and nobody made any kind of noise. Cody sat back down on his mattress and looked up to the ceiling. He saw cockroaches coming out through the heating duct and hoped they would stay up there and wouldn't come down toward him.

Soon, the lights went out and everything was dark, except for one beam of moonlight shining in through the room's single small, bare window

Cody was tired but had nothing to cover up with. He kept thinking about the damn roaches, and he was sweating from the heat blowing in from the vent. He dozed off only to be awakened by something crawling all over his body. He jumped up, slapping cockroaches on his body. They had been trying to drink the sweat from his skin. The cockroaches retreated, running back up the walls to the heating vent.

He yelled for the guards, but he got no response. So, he stood by the door all night until morning, refusing to lie back down on the mattress. *This is why people are fucking crazy here. They have to put up with shit like this*, he thought. Then he thought about the guy across the hall, the one they had shot up with that shit. He was passed out over there and must have a room filled with those fucking roaches, too.

The next morning, they served breakfast on a paper plate through the door and gave them nothing to eat the shit with. Some crazy-looking retards passed out the food, and Cody again thought to himself, *there is no fucking way I am going to eat this shit or take a crap in that bucket either.*

What a fucking hellhole this place is, Cody thought. He decided to sleep during the daytime and stay up at night so the cockroaches would not crawl on him. Nobody came to the room all weekend. When Monday morning came around, they sent two state troopers to pick him up and take him back to court. Cody felt great to get a ride out of that fucking nut house. He already had a plan to jump out of the courthouse window if the judge tried to send him back there for another thirty days.

When he stood in front of the judge this time, his court-appointed attorney first addressed the deplorable conditions Cody dealt with over the weekend and stated his client felt he was competent to stand trial. The judge ordered a court-appointed shrink to evaluate him at the courthouse. Within three hours, the judge sent Cody to a house of correction to await his trial.

Cody was relieved not to go back to the nut house. He knew his trial would take about nine months to a year. He also knew he didn't have a chance of walking away from it, but he hoped to get the charges dropped down to a lesser charge or maybe even get the charges dropped to self-defense. He planned to challenge the size and weight of Maria's dad and compare his state of mind. The old man was really drunk that night, and Cody would claim he'd feared for his life.

Cody knew he had to devise a plan to beat the charges somehow and not get sent to prison for the rest of his life. He met with his attorney once a month, and they went over and over how everything happened. The attorney told Cody he would try to get the court to drop the charges down to manslaughter, but there was no way he could get him off on self-defense because of the way Cody shot the guy. Cody told him to try anyway.

Chapter Seven

Cody knew one thing about being jailed: you couldn't trust anybody because they would sell you out for anything. Cody hung with a couple of people, but he never talked about much. He got great enjoyment out of listening to other inmates talk about their crimes, both what they were in jail for and what they'd done in the past.

What fucking dopes these guys are, bragging about all the shit they've done, Cody thought. They could get more time for running their mouths if someone ratted them out.

But listening to their bullshit and working out every night in the gym kept him amused and helped the time pass. He accepted the reality of his situation and started to prepare for when he would go up to the state prison to do some hard time for killing Maria's father, that fucker.

He received a lot of letters from Johnny and Danny. They sent him cash all the time and kept him updated on the shit that was going on the outside. Then, after about five months the letters stopped coming. He found out Johnny and Danny were busted for an armed robbery and were being held in a jail in Boston jail. They, too, would be heading up to the state prison as soon as they went to trial.

Jail was the same old shit every day. Cody soon realized nobody gave a shit about someone once they went to jail. And why should they? People only needed him when he was out there helping them make money. Then one day, to his amazement, he received a letter from his girlfriend Maria. As he read it, he was shocked. In the letter she told him she felt bad and how sorry she and her family were that this had happened. She told Cody she had felt something was going to happen that night and that she did in fact hate her father. She wanted her father to hurt for all the bad things he'd done to their family in the past. Cody wanted to use her letter during his trial and hoped it would get him a manslaughter sentence, which would only require him to serve less than ten years.

Cody sat in his cell, fighting with his thoughts about the few girls he knew and had messed around with long before he met Maria. He had never had any feeling toward them. Maria had changed everything in such a short time. Everything had been going fine for him until he met her. She was someone he actually cared about, which was totally new to him. Maria had a pretty face and a wonderful smile, and he listened to her every word. Cody had a reality check about loving someone. He was not use to loving anything, but hate … that was easier for him. Hate was all he'd understood growing up in the streets. He learned to fight his way up in life from an early age. Hate was a lot easier for him than loving another person.

He thought about Maria's father and the stories she'd told him about how he used to hit her and her mother when she was growing up and how she was scared of him all the time. When Cody first started liking her, he knew he would protect her no matter what, and that had led to all of this. Cody felt no remorse for his actions but at the same time felt guilty for falling in love with Maria. So he never wrote back to her and burned the letter. The next time he saw Maria was in court. She had to testify against him and relate what he had done to her father that night. That was the beginning of his trial.

The trial itself only lasted only four days. People took the stand and talked about this and that and whatever. What surprised Cody the most was the coroner's testimony. The man said the first bullet that hit Maria's father killed him. Cody was shocked. *I never should have fired those other two shots.*

The coroner explained that when a small bullet, like one from the .22 pistol Cody used that night, entered the body, it bounced off the bones and couldn't go anywhere

"The first bullet hit Mr. Canella in the shoulder and ripped down past through his heart and stopped in his rib cage, killing him instantly," the coroner said. "The second bullet hit his chest and went through the heart again, landing in his kidney. The third bullet was removed from his temple of his brain."

Cody remembered the look on Maria's father's face that night. He just sat there and stared into Cody's eyes after the first shot. Cody hadn't realized he was already dead from the first bullet.

As the trial continued, things started to look bad for Cody. The district attorney's office pushed for a first degree murder case, which meant life with no parole. Halfway through the trial, Cody's attorney went to the district attorney and asked for a plea. He requested a manslaughter plea with an eighteen- to twenty-year sentence, of which Cody would only have to serve twelve. But because it was an election year and he was a prick, the district attorney only offered life in the second degree, which meant life, but Cody would be eligible to see the parole board after fifteen years.

It was a tough decision for Cody. He knew he would be going away to prison no matter what, but did he want to gamble with his life and take a chance on a verdict from the jury? Cody knew he could take the stand and try to convince the jury of the situation the night of the murder, but he wouldn't be able to explain why he carried around a gun. If he fucked it up, he would end up with first degree murder, which meant he would die in prison without parole. He was running out of time. *It's only fifteen years. It's only fifteen years*, he repeated over and over in his mind. He knew he would have a shot of getting out down the road somehow.

So that was it. He'd gone from starting his shit at twelve years of age to being seventeen and pleading guilty to second degree murder. The judge accepted his plea, and the jury was released.

"Hey kid, you're young," one the court officers said as they led Cody back to his cell. "Fifteen years is not forever. You'll have a shot of getting out someday."

Cody was numb. He couldn't feel anything or hear straight. *Fucking life and fifteen years. How am I going to do fifteen fucking years?* Cody thought. But he had been smart to take the deal and what little hope it offered for his future instead of gambling with the chance of dying of old age in prison.

As Cody sat in the back jail cell of the court room, he decided right there and then that prison would not hold him. He would be free again somehow. He had to get in touch with Johnny. He had grown up with Johnny and trusted him with his life. Johnny would be in one of the three Massachusetts prisons, and Cody knew he would help him at all costs.

Chapter Eight

It only took two hours to process all of the paperwork, and then Cody was handcuffed in the back of a cruiser heading to the big house—the state's maximum security prison, home of every fucking murderer and psychopath in the state of Massachusetts. Once there, the prison officials stripped him down and took pictures of his tattoos and other marks on his body. They took more mug shots and wanted to know everyone he knew. Of course, Cody told them nothing. He didn't know anyone and was just there to do his time and mind his own business. Yeah right. They didn't believe that. But the guards didn't give a fuck about anything. They just wanted to make it out of the prison every day alive and go home to their families.

Cody soon found out he had to stay in the new-man section in the hospital unit for a few days until a cell opened up in population. He was fine with that. He planned to get his contacts together within the prison. One thing about prison and prisoners was the inmates knew everything before it happened, and they knew who and where everybody was at any time.

Some of the convicts that knew Cody from the streets, and even other kids he'd grown up with inside the DYS, were in that same prison. They knew what time he would arrive and were looking forward to seeing him. They hoped he would team up with their groups. They knew he had a good reputation and that he was a stand up guy and not a rat.

Within two hours after Cody was put in his cell, other inmates sent him down smokes, books, and drugs as a welcome to the big house kind of thing, all things he could use if he needed to take the edge off, relax, and reflect on where he was now. He had heard about prison from guys on the street that had done time before. They always told him that everybody was for themselves, not to trust anyone, and to only count on himself. So Cody kept all of that in mind. Two days later, he moved up into population and was placed in cellblock four.

As it turns out, Cody didn't know anybody in that block. It held about sixty inmates and had three tiers of twenty cells. All the cells were single-man cells. He went to his cell on the second tier, tired and needing a shower. He grabbed his towel and headed for the single shower located at the end of each tier. As he showered, he kept looking out from behind the curtain. He saw a few black guys waiting out in the doorway. They were talking shit about getting them a nice white ass to tap. He thought the fucking boneheads wanted to try to rape his ass.

He dried off quickly and walked by them, showing no fear. He headed toward his cell, knowing they were checking him out. He dressed fast, and within a couple of minutes, a white inmate he'd never met walked up to his cell. The guy introduced himself as Duke and said he was a friend of Eddie and Pat. He handed Cody a shank, the prison term for a knife.

"If these fucking boneheads try any shit, I've got your back," he told Cody. It turned out that Duke had gotten word from Pat and Eddie that Cody was coming into his block. The shank was from a few of Cody's old friends. "Use it only if you need to, but keep it close at all times," Duke advised. He then told Cody the guys would meet him in the mess hall at lunchtime.

Then he said, "Fuck this. Follow me and put the shank under your shirt." He walked right up to the boneheads, who still stood outside the shower stall and addressed them all at once, "He is with me and our group, and if you fuck with him, you're all fucking going to die. Do you fucking get it?"

They backed down quickly. "Yes, we get it. We don't want any trouble. Everything's cool."

Then Duke turned to Cody and shouted in front of everyone

there, "It don't matter if they are white, black, or whatever, if you think somebody is even looking at you the wrong way, act on it quick and be ready to kill the motherfuckers at all times in here. Take no shit from anyone."

Cody just nodded and smiled. Soon lunchtime came.

"Let's go," Duke said and walked Cody down into the lunch hall.

Cody went to stand in line.

"What the fuck are you doing?" Duke asked him

"What are you talking about?" Cody said.

"Only the losers wait in fucking line," Duke yelled and then escorted him up to the front of the line.

They got their food, and Duke took him over to a set of three tables filled with guys dressed a little better than most of the inmates in the mess hall. Cody saw Pat and Eddie, the guys he knew from the streets, the ones who killed the police dog. They jumped up, yelling to Cody, "Welcome to the big house!" They introduced him to their friends.

Pat and Eddie had a good thing going there in the prison. They were working for the wise guys who ran the booking and loan shark operations for all bets within the prison. Inmates paid in cigarettes, drugs, and cash.

They planned to pull Cody out of block four but then thought it would be better to keep him there and have him work and learn the ropes of prison life from Duke. Duke was serving a life sentence for a killing six people during a house invasion and already had ten years under his belt. He knew prison was his life and he was going to die there. He seemed to be an okay guy, but he was a fucking junkie. He was from Cambridge and loved to laugh and shoot drugs in his arm. He carried a needle around all the time and shot up five times a day. Cody didn't get it. It seemed the whole fucking prison population was high all fucking day and night.

Even Eddie and Pat had changed, though they'd only been in the system a year or two. They were not the same guys he'd known on the streets. Cody wondered if that shit was going to happen to him. He loved to drink and smoke pot, but he didn't want to stick fucking needles in his arms and get hooked on that shit.

Cody did his thing and hung with the older Irish gangsters from Southie and Charlestown in the prison yard. He liked to hear their stories. It helped the time move a little faster. After about nine months in the maximum prison, because he was one of the youngest inmates there and he stayed out of trouble, they let him transfer down to a medium security prison. The older inmates where happy for him. They told Cody to look up different people when he got there. They had already sent word down to their friends that he was coming and to look out for him. They would have his back if there was a problem.

As a younger inmate in the prison system, Cody was a lucky kid. People liked him and knew what he had done on the streets. He had made a little name for himself in the short time he spent in the maximum security prison. The old timers ran the prisons better than the correction personnel. Cody met some real gangsters in there, guys from the old mob. If someone crossed them with just a few words, that person and even that person's family on the outside would be dead on their command.

Those guys had the real power within the prison walls, but Cody also remembered it from the street. All of those wise guys had power as well, and they sold out their own people to get it. They were all fucking rats. He would never forget how those bastards grew to power and how the people around them had their heads up their asses and made them look more powerful than they were.

Chapter Nine

Cody was transferred to the new medium security prison, and everybody there was about his age and not much older. Word quickly got around that Cody was somebody who knew people and he wasn't someone to fuck with. People knew if they fucked with him, something would happen to them somewhere down the road.

He couldn't believe how many people he knew there. He had done time with more than half of the prison's population as a juvenile in the DYS. He felt like he was back home in his own element, a big difference from the maximum security prison he had just left. His two street partners were there, too—Johnny and Danny. They had both picked up three to five years for some bullshit robbery.

The first thing Cody did was talk to Danny and Johnny about how he was getting the fuck out of prison. He was not going to do fifteen years and live like all of the asshole junkies. Danny and Johnny only had another two to three years before they could move on to pre-release centers, but they promised Cody once they were out, they would do anything to help get him out. Cody knew their word was good.

They were like brothers and very loyal to each other. Danny and Johnny gave Cody a lot of hope, and it kept him going. He knew they always had his back and they never lied to each other. Cody worked in the prison store where inmates used their own money to get food, soap, cigarettes, and stuff like that. It was a dream job every inmate wanted, but they either had to be someone or know someone to run a prison store. Cody was there three months and walked into that job.

The prison system was not very hard for the officials to run. It ran itself. Hell, they had a program called furloughs in the prison system. The inmates would go out on a furlough for twenty-four or forty-eight hours and got to be with their families, wives, or girlfriends and then return to do their time. Inmates in the program received furloughs every three months under good behavior. But there was a catch to it. They had to be within certain guidelines and not have much time left on their sentences. Cody was fucked. He had a life sentence, going on three years now, with a lot more to go.

Cody lived inside the medium security prison with thirty-foot walls and an outside prison farm. The prison had no prison cells. Instead it had rooms with doors that the guards locked at night. It held about fifteen hundred or more prisoners and was nothing compared to the maximum security prison Cody had just left. His door was unlocked at seven in the morning, and he had to be back in the room by nine. He could roam anywhere within the prison and all he needed was a pass from a guard to go any place inside the walls. The guards were always accountable for prisoners in whatever section of the prison they entered. That was how they kept their count of inmates.

Each floor held about fifty inmates, and Cody associated and dealt with most of them with the exception of blacks. There was one rule concerning blacks: Never trust those motherfuckers. They would sell you down the river quicker than anyone, and if you fought them you should hit them in the knees. They had very weak knees. Never hit them in the head because you'd hurt your hands. That was why they were all called boneheads. The blacks hated Cody and his friends as much as Cody hated them.

Cody stayed in shape and was always ready for anything. He still had a lot of anger built up inside of him and worked out on the punching bag every day and sometimes boxed at the prison gym. He was 5' 7" and weighed 155 lbs. He hit with such authority that he almost felt sorry for any guy that came up against him. One day, Cody was sparring in the ring and a bonehead jumped into the ring with him. He boxed southpaw. Cody had never fought anyone who fought southpaw. The guy packed a power punch with his left hand like Cody did with his right. The guy kept hitting and hitting blow after blow to Cody's face until Cody went down on the mat, nearly knocked out.

The guy was a far better boxer than Cody and knocked him down and out in no time. As Cody lay on the mat, waiting to regain his balance, he knew he was beat and felt embarrassed that the fucking bonehead just walked in and fucked him up. Johnny helped Cody get back to his room. He felt a little fucked-up about letting the bonehead light Cody up, but Cody felt good about the beating he'd taken from the black son of a bitch. It was the first time he had felt real pain, a hurt pain, and he liked the feeling it gave him. Nobody had ever put an ass whipping on him like that before. He would have great pleasure when the time came to get that bonehead back. He smiled as he washed away the dried up blood from his face and went to bed.

Inmates throughout the prison talked about the beating Cody took that day. Cody just smiled and said, "You can't win them all." Johnny and Danny asked Cody what he wanted to do. Cody smiled and said nothing.

"I need you guys out on the streets to help me get the fuck out of here. I'll deal with this at another time," he told them. They agreed and backed off. They always let Cody call the shots. They trusted him because he tried to think with a clear head all the time.

Later that month, Cody met up with the bonehead in the weight room. The guy was lying on his back, benching about 225 lbs. Seeing that nobody was around, Cody wrapped a five-pound weight in his towel, walked over to him, and started smashing him in the face with the weight. The weights the guy was benching fell hard upon his chest, and he rolled off the bench press. Cody continued to hit him. Soon the guy's brains were showing through his forehead. Cody leaned over and whispered in his ear, "I hope you can hear me, motherfucker. This is what you get for kicking my ass."

The guards found the guy later. He wasn't dead, but he would never know his own name again. He was a fucking vegetable. Everybody heard how they had to dig the guy's teeth out of his throat, not to mention put his brains back into his head. Danny and Johnny heard what happened and looked at Cody in the mess hall.

"Feel better now?" Johnny asked.

Cody smiled. "A lot better than the other guy."

Whenever anything happened within prison walls, it was just a part of life. The guards cleaned up the mess, asked a few questions, and then life went on like it never happened and everybody waited for something else to happen. Violence in prisons added a spice of excitement to the environment and gave everyone something to talk about. Nobody wanted to be the victim, but everybody got off on it. It even gave the guards stories to tell one another and their families when they went home at night. And just when they thought they had seen it all, something new happened.

After that first boxing match with the bonehead, another guy was stupid enough to step in the ring with Cody just to spar. Cody had sworn never to go down again. He had the guy on the ropes and beat him so badly that he was holding the guy upright with his left glove and beating him with his right. The guy tried to just fall out through the ropes, but Cody gave him one more shot in the jaw, and the guy flew down and out of the ring.

Everyone thought Cody killed him. The air was as silent as death for a few seconds. The other inmate's blood was everywhere. Cody lifted his gloves to his face and smelled the blood. He looked over to Danny and Johnny and gave them a little smile that said it all. Johnny knew Cody was still one angry son of a bitch and that he thirsted for other humans' blood. Cody wanted others to suffer inside like he suffered. From the smile on Cody's face, Johnny knew Cody hated the fucking world more now than he ever had before.

Cody did not have many visitors from the outside world. His mom came once every three months or so and visited him whenever she could get a ride. She had never been there for him as a kid, but on her visits she asked him to get his life together and talked about how she wanted him to get out someday. But Cody didn't want to hear any more of that crap and told her that prison was his life now and to stop visiting him. He knew he had to stop dealing with people from the outside world. They just came to visit and talked about stuff he had no control over. He didn't want to live up to their expectations and dreams of him getting out of prison.

They knew nothing about prison and what went on there. So, at that time in his life he chose not to receive any more visits from his family or people from outside the prison walls. He accepted prison for what it was and did not want any ties, feelings, or emotions from anybody. He returned to his room to get on with his life.

Regardless of what went on in prison, Cody was still the new guy with only four years under his belt. The few real gangsters there still ran everything inside. The prison superintendent—they nicknamed him the Greek—had full say on who did what and who went where, but he got along very well with the old school gangsters. They had him in their pockets.

The superintendent let them out on furloughs every three months and stuffed their money into his pockets all of the time. He was as corrupt as they were. Cody asked a favor of one of the old timers to see if they could help him get the superintendent to him to move out onto the prison farm. They said they'd look into it and get back to him. A few months went by and it happened. The superintendent approved Cody to move out to the farm. A million things ran through Cody's twenty one year old mind. It was his big chance to get the fuck out of prison, take off, and be free

Johnny and Danny couldn't believe it. They told Cody they would make it up to see him in a month or so and to keep his cool for now. Cody only had four years in and he was being placed outside the walls to go milk fucking cows. There were other lifers up on the farm, but most of them had put over ten years in and weren't a threat of running off. Most of them were fucking informants anyway. The guards were not at all happy about Cody being sent up to the farm, but they did not run the prison.

Chapter Ten

The farm was up on a hill outside the prison. It held around one hundred inmates, two men to a room. They placed Cody with an inmate named Richardson. He was a big-time informant for the guards and the prison administration. Cody knew the asshole was there to keep an eye on him, but Cody had to keep his cool and keep one step ahead of him. Richardson's job was to show Cody the ropes of the farm and all the rules he had to follow.

The farm worked to help supplement the prison. They milked cows, fed chickens, and worked in the hayfields and miles of vegetable gardens. They even butchered the cows and chickens to feed everyone down in the prison. Cody knew nothing about farm work—he was a city boy—but he had his choice of the jobs he wanted. He chose to milk cows, which meant he had to get up every morning at 3 AM, go down to a barn with ten other inmates, and hook up machines to milk the fucking cows. He had to pick up their shit, too, but he dealt with it twice a day.

Cody had to learn very fast about how the farm worked and how the hell he could get out of there and back to the streets. Everybody else living on the farm was content and did the same thing each day. Cody could not understand it and wondered why the inmates would just sit back and do their time. Some of the guys had some big-time to do and were not getting out anytime soon. Anyone could just up and leave the place with just a ride.

Danny and Johnny made it up to the farm a couple of weeks later. They were both heading out to a pre-release within the next thirty days. At the pre-release center, they would work on the streets every day and would have to be back at a certain time every night and sometimes be required to take a random drug test. It was cool, and Cody kept reminding the both of them how he had to get the fuck out of prison and it was not for him. Johnny told Cody to chill out, wait for him to get out, and give him time to get his own shit together. He told Cody to hang in there and not to take off until then. Cody told him he would try.

Most people Cody associated with wanted exactly what he did—to live a fast life with no rules and to do whatever they wanted. Danny and Johnny had a short stay on the farm and moved on to the pre-release center a couple of weeks later. Before they left, they again reminded Cody to relax. Once they got out of pre-release, they would set things up for him and they would all be together again, doing their own thing.

Cody managed to get a new roommate, a guy named Dennis. He was a biker who belonged to a big biker gang called the Devil's Demons or something like that. Cody had some dealings with Dennis inside the walls for drugs. Bikers always got the good drugs into the prison system because they had their biker chicks to do whatever they wanted.

Cody never wanted to be a biker or have any part of those guys, but he learned how very organized they were and how they had a brotherhood of gang members that took care of anything. They weren't gangsters or mobsters, just a bunch of guys who were some bad motherfuckers when they had to be, with old ladies who would kill for them if they just said the word.

Cody was very impressed and learned more about the bikers and how they worked. He and Dennis formed a small bond.

"You're not going to hit me with any weights are ya?" was the first thing Dennis said to Cody once he got settled in the room.

They laughed, lit a joint, and told each other stories from the streets. Dennis was able to feel Cody out and knew he didn't want to be there. Dennis only had nine months left and had to finish up his time.

"If you want, I can hook you up with a ride out of here anytime you want," he told Cody.

"I'd like that, but I don't have anywhere to go once I get out, Cody said.

"I can hook you up if you'll consider doing me a favor while you're out there," Dennis said.

Cody thought about his offer for a few days. *Why not take Dennis up on this offer? How bad of a favor could he want?* He knew Dennis was a stand up person. He wasn't a rat, and bikers took care of their own shit. So, Cody asked Dennis what he wanted done.

Dennis told him he wanted an outsider like Cody to toss a couple of hand grenades into another biker gang's hangout and that it had to be an outsider and not someone from his gang. Cody didn't ask questions and told Dennis to set up a ride and tell him how and when he wanted it done.

Dennis told Cody everything would be set up through his old lady and once Cody was out, she would handle all the details. They set the date for Cody's ride for two weeks later on a Friday night. They would do it right when visiting hours were over, that way it would be dark out and there would be plenty of cars coming and going. The guards wouldn't know Cody was gone until the 11:00 PM count took place.

Chapter Eleven

That Friday came. It started to get dark, and around 9:00 PM. Cody grabbed some clothes and about three hundred in cash and took off through the back door. He hauled ass down toward Route 4. Near the south gate, he climbed the little fence where he was supposed to wait for a red car with its high beams on. It was supposed to be there at 9:10 PM on the money.

Bingo. Cody spotted the car driving slowly toward him and made himself visible. As the car came to a stop, the girl driving smiled. "You need a ride, stranger?" she asked and then laughed.

He jumped in the back. His heart was racing. Sweat dripped off him as he lay down on the seat.

"My name is Cindy," she said. "Here's a little present for you." She tossed him a loaded .45 automatic. "Stay down and enjoy the ride, and let's hope you will not be using that on anyone tonight."

She then turned up the radio and headed up to a yacht club north of Boston in a small town called Medford. It took about an hour and a half to get there. She walked Cody into the cabin of a forty-foot boat that was docked there.

"Here's your home for the weekend. Nobody will bother you here. Just get some sleep and I'll be back tomorrow before noon to pick you up."

Cody went straight for the TV set and turned it on for the news, thinking his escape would be all over the news stations, but there was nothing about him. He thought maybe it would be on tomorrow because it was late. He grabbed a bottle of whiskey from a nearby cabinet and drank himself to sleep, holding his gun in his hand.

The next day, Cindy picked him up and took him to her place. He grabbed a quick shower and some food. She told him it might take up to three weeks to make the bombing happen. They had to make sure two key rival members were at the meeting. Then he was supposed to toss the grenades on the two rival gang members as they started their bikes to leave the meeting. Once it was done, Dennis's gang would help get Cody across the border into Canada, and then he would be on his own.

"Whatever," Cody said and smiled. "I need to have some fun."

She took him to a biker bar. When Cody walked in, everybody looked at him strangely. Then out of nowhere, a biker shouted over the bar.

"Is that fucking Cody? Come here, you little bastard." He picked Cody up, still yelling, "When the fuck did you get out?" As the biker picked him up in excitement, Cody's gun fell on the floor.

The biker was another guy Cody knew from the joint named Wayne. He was a big bastard with long blond hair and dumb as a doornail. He carried Cody up to the bar, and they began to drink and talk about prison. Cody told Wayne he had just escaped the night before and was a little fucked up in the head at that moment.

Wayne smiled and looked at Cody. "Well then, we got to get you laid," he exclaimed.

"You're right on the money there, my friend," Cody said.

Another biker walked up to Cody and handed him his gun. He tucked it away. Cody then told Cindy he was going with Wayne and would call her for updates to follow through with the bargain he made with Dennis.

She leaned in close to Cody. "Make sure you do," she whispered and then licked his ear with her tongue. "We have people everywhere."

With that, she left and they went off to party. Wayne told Cody he could crash with him if he wanted and that he'd help in any way he could. Cody took him up on his offer. He knew he would need a place to hang and rides when he wanted to get places.

Cody had to make some calls and contact some of his old friends. But who? Just about everybody he knew was doing prison time. Then he remembered Dave, his old probation officer who—in Cody's mind—would owe him for the rest of his life. Cody made a few calls and got Dave's number. He found out his buddy Dave had moved up the food chain and was now working for some influential people in the State House in Boston. When Cody called him, Dave was shocked to hear from him.

"When and how did you get out?"

Because Dave didn't know anything, Cody lied to him and told him that he was out on a furlough from prison for two-day and needed to talk to him. Dave agreed to meet with him the next day for lunch. They met at the Park Street Station in Boston, and Dave was very happy to see him. They went to lunch and talked about Dave's new job with the attorney general's office.

"So how did you get into the furlough program after only being in four to five years?" Dave asked Cody. "I heard you received a big sentence for shooting someone."

"Yes, I did get put away with a big sentence," Cody told Dave. He sat back in his chair, took a sip of his drink, and calmly looked Dave in the eye. "Stay calm. I want to tell you something."

Dave sat back, looking confused. Cody explained how he had received a life sentence and that he'd just escape from the prison work farm. Dave's jaw nearly hit the floor. He leaned over the table. His eyes looked like they were ready to pop out of his head.

"Get the fuck out of here. Are you fucking with me?" Dave whispered loudly. He began to have a fucking panic attack. "I work for the fucking attorney general's office. We put people in prison. I can't be seen with you under these circumstances. Do you know how fucked I would be if I were seen with you right now?

"I understand," Cody told him. "But I need your help right now and might need it more down the road." Dave continued to be apprehensive. Cody leaned over the table. "Look, stop being an asshole," he told Dave very quietly. "I need help from you right now. When you needed my help, I never questioned you. I jumped in your car and went to New York to kill some son of a bitch for you, and let's not even talk about all the cocaine I gave you to blow up your nose. I'm sure you still have that habit."

Dave stood and took a step back. He took a deep breath, knowing Cody had him by the balls. Cody had too much shit on him, and his tracks could be traced over the time they had known each other. Dave knew that Cody could ruin his career at any given moment and that if he did, he could even be jailed himself.

"What do you need?" Dave asked.

Cody sprung up from his chair. "The first thing will be some money and some good IDs, and I need them fast."

"I can get you two grand now, and I'll make a call over to someone in the Motor Vehicle Department," Dave said. "I have a friend over there that will set you up with a photo identification license tomorrow and ask no questions."

They left the restaurant and walked up to the bank. After they left the bank, Dave handed Cody the money.

"We can't meet anymore. I have to protect myself and my future," Dave explained.

"We are friends, but if I ever need something down the road, I'll have to contact you discretely," Cody told Dave. "I have to be able to count on you, and I have to know you'll be there for me."

Dave promised he would be, but very reluctantly. As they shook hands, Cody gripped Dave's very tightly and pulled him closer. "Never forget the past because it always comes back to bite you in the ass. See you again someday, my friend," he said and went on his way.

The next day Cody went to the DMV and got his new license. They gave him a name that was hard to spell, but it would cover him in case he ever got stopped.

Next, Cody had to find a way to contact Johnny and Danny over in the pre-release center in Boston and let them know he escaped. He knew they would help him out.

Chapter Twelve

Now that he had escaped, Cody was paranoid. He looked around all the time because he was a wanted man and did not know who to trust or where to turn. It bothered him that nothing about his escape was on the news, but he knew the Department of Correction was probably covering his escape up because they wouldn't be able to justify placing a lifer with only four years in on the farm. Some people's asses would be hung out to dry because of his escape.

He knew he could not go back to his old neighborhoods or be seen around town. The Boston cops knew his face. So, he had Wayne drive, and he kept his head down when he went to Boston. They drove into the city around 5:00 AM and had the balls to sit in a parking lot outside the pre-release center in Mattapan to wait for Danny or Johnny to walk out.

Sure enough, out walked Johnny, half asleep and heading toward the bus stop. They pulled up beside him, and Cody shouted at him out the window. "Hey, Johnny boy, you need a ride somewhere?"

Johnny looked over in disbelief and did a double take. He couldn't believe it was Cody. A big smile appeared on his face. He jumped into the car and off they went. It was the best feeling they'd had in a long time. They were back on the streets together. They had to come up with a plan that would work to cover Johnny until he got out of the pre-release center.

"Where's Danny?" Cody asked Johnny. "He could help us."

"Danny got sent back to the prison and is looking at more time because he got caught stealing some shit," Johnny told him.

"An undercover cop was standing right beside him. The guy tried to grab Danny and a fight was on. Danny didn't even know he was a cop."

Johnny left the pre-release center every morning at 5:00 AM and didn't have to be back until 6:00 PM for check. Then, after check he could leave again and return at 10:00 PM. On weekends, he could say he was going to stay with his family and not return until Sunday night. All they did at the center was make sure the inmates stayed off drugs by giving them pee tests at random times.

Nobody ever checked if they were working in the daytime. They just had to show the officials they were putting money in their bank accounts every week. So, Cody had Wayne pick Johnny up every morning, and they started robbing stores in the daytime and had Johnny back to the center on time in the evening. Cody figured he had nothing to lose, and he promised himself he would always do whatever he wanted, whether he got caught or not.

"I'm glad I didn't bother waiting on you and Danny to help break me out from the prison farm," Cody told Johnny one day.

"I would have been there for you," Johnny shouted. "Remember, you're my brother, and don't ever forget that, Cody." After a few moments, Johnny asked Cody how he had gotten out.

Cody told him about the deal he made with Dennis and how he got a ride off the prison farm. Johnny was not happy about it.

"You are way out of your element," Johnny said. "Fuck them bikers. You don't need to get involved with that shit. Let those bikers do their own dirty work and start their own wars with each other. You're free now, and we are partners to the end, so let's do what we do best. If you do this for them, do you really think they will help get you out of the country into Canada? They will drive you up there and bury you in the ground somewhere near the border."

Cody thought about what Johnny said. He was right. The bikers would bury him and nobody would ever know or miss him. That was exactly what Cody needed to hear. He knew Johnny could always get his mind back on the right track. They had grown up together and believed in each other. Johnny also thought it would be best to get rid of Wayne for a while because he was part of the biker scene. Wayne was fine with it and told Cody to call if he needed anything.

Johnny set Cody up with Jane, one of his old girlfriends. She had her own car and her own place. She met Cody and instantly fell in love. She was the kind of chick that got off on hanging with criminals and loved to get into trouble. Cody couldn't care less. He was getting laid and had someone to drive him around and a place to stay. Plus, he and Johnny could hang out together just like the old times. Jane had a nice place right in the heart of Boston, near the Back Bay. Cody didn't want to be in Boston, but he thought if he didn't do anything there, it would be fine.

Soon enough, Cody started to forget he was on the run from prison and that he'd only been out for a couple of months. At times, he forgot there were cops looking for him. He didn't care. He needed money to survive. Cody would just walk into any random place at any time, pull out his gun, and take the cash. He pulled fast armed robberies for small cash. He got off on it and loved it.

While Jane waited up the street, Cody would walk in any store, bold as could be, pull out his gun, go up to the clerk, and ask him, "You don't want to get shot today, do you?" The clerks would give him the cash, and he would make them lie on the floor and count to one hundred while he walked out like he just paid for a pack of smokes.

Johnny drew up a plan to rob a supermarket in Weymouth over a long holiday weekend. They knew the big supermarkets always had big cash on hand. The store's money was picked up by armored trucks on Tuesday mornings. Supermarkets were better than banks for hard cash. Cody and Johnny figured if they hit a big score, they would not have to keep doing the small shit for five hundred dollars here and there and would be able to get the hell out of Massachusetts for a while and lay low.

The only thing that bothered Cody about their plan was after they hit the supermarket, they would have to go through a small city called Quincy to get to the main highway. Every crook in Massachusetts knew Quincy had a system at its police station that if a place got robbed, someone in the station would hit a button and all of the fifteen stoplights on the major streets would turn red, which then clogged up all of the traffic lanes. If they went the opposite direction out of Weymouth, it was all country roads that all led to the ocean. So, they knew they had to go through Quincy, and they had to be sure they beat all the lights.

It was snowing lightly on the day of the robbery. Johnny stole a car and he and Cody followed Jane's car up to the supermarket in Weymouth. The plan was simple: Jane would wait in a parking lot a mile away from the supermarket, and Cody and Johnny would walk into the supermarket, look for the manager, and demand he open the safe. They would put the money in shopping bags and walk out.

They walked into the supermarket. Without a mask on, Cody walked up to the store manager and told him he had a shotgun under his coat and that the store was being robbed. He advised the man not to do anything stupid because there were three other guys in the store that would start shooting people. Johnny stood over near the office with a cap rolled down to cover his face.

The manager unlocked the office. The two women doing office work inside looked up and saw the masked Johnny and Cody holding a gun to the manager's head. They started acting like drama queens. One held her chest and the other passed out on her desk. Nobody wanted to open the safe. Johnny pulled back the hammer of his gun and yelled, "Five seconds and someone is going to die for money that doesn't belong to you." He aimed

the gun at the lady holding her chest and started to count, "One
... two ..."

"Stop," the manager pleaded. He leaned over and opened the
safe.

Cody grabbed as much money as he could fit into two big
brown shopping bags, handed them to Johnny, and told him to
go to the car. As Johnny walked out of the office, he rolled up
his mask, which made it look like a hat again, and walked out of
the store.

Cody ripped the phone wire and the store speaker wires out of
the wall and told them there were two other guys in the store that
would shoot anyone who left the office before five minutes passed.
He then walked out of the office and jumped into the car with
Johnny. They drove over to where Jane was waiting with the second
car. Cody placed the money in the back seat and both he and Johnny
lay down in the back seat so they could not be seen. They knew the
police would be looking for at least two guys for sure, maybe four.

Jane was all hyped up like she was having an orgasm. They
kept telling her to drive the normal speed and not any faster.
They just needed to make it through Quincy and they would
all home free. Just as they passed the last light in Quincy, Jane
looked in the mirror and saw the lights turn and all traffic stop.
Blue lights started flashing everywhere.

They got on the highway, happy as pigs in shit, knowing they
should get back to Jane's apartment so they could count up all
the cash. Cody thought they had about sixty to eighty thousand
dollars or more.

"We should get the hell out of this state and chill somewhere
warm for a while," Johnny told Cody.

"What and stop having all this fun?" Cody said, reminding
Johnny how they had pulled off the score so easily.

Johnny laughed. "We have to be smart and lay low. We have
enough money here to last awhile. We should go down to Florida
and kick back."

Cody agreed.

Chapter Thirteen

Their adrenaline was pumping as they pulled up in front of Jane's apartment. They could not wait to start counting the money. Johnny stepped out on the left side of the car and grabbed the bags. Cody got out of the other side, took off his overcoat, and hid the sawed off shotgun under his coat. He grabbed the other guns and stuck them in the waistband of his pants.

When he turned, he noticed an older guy sitting across the street on a stair stoop, reading a newspaper. Cody felt like something was out of place.

"Let's go," Johnny yelled. "Jane has to drive down the street and turn around to park in her parking space in the back alleyway."

They entered Jane's first floor apartment, and Johnny knelt down and poured the money onto the floor.

"Let's start counting this shit up," he called out with excitement and then looked up at Cody. "What the fuck is wrong with you?"

"Something's wrong, very wrong," Cody said. "This is the back bay of Boston. It's too quiet. I don't even hear a fucking car off the main street."

Johnny listened. "You're right. It's too goddamn quiet," he said. "Where's Jane? She should have parked the car by now."

Cody remembered the fucking guy sitting on the stoop. He ran over to the window and peeked through the closed blinds. He saw two well-dressed guys trying to pick the lock to the front door. "It's the cops," he yelled. As he turned to warn Johnny he ripped down the metal blinds, making a lot of noise. The two cops looked at Cody and drew their guns. They ran to take cover behind the cars parked on the street.

Cody stepped out of the window, and he and Johnny grabbed their guns. They ran across the hallway and kicked in the door to the apartment across the hall. They opened the window, prepared to jump into the alleyway and run, but they stopped and looked out. There were nearly twenty state police cars lined up in the alleyway. Two troopers had their shotguns pointed right at them.

"Stop!" the troopers yelled.

Cody pulled Johnny back to the floor. "We're fucked now," he said.

They ran back to Jane's place and locked the door. They looked at each other.

"How do you want to handle this?" Johnny asked.

Cody shook his head, grabbed a couple of bottles of whiskey. "Here, start drinking," he said and tossed his gun to the floor.

Johnny stared at all the money. "How did they know to come here? We weren't followed. We got a clean getaway from the supermarket."

Just then, they heard the floorboards outside the apartment door creak. Johnny wedged himself between the refrigerator and the wall, not wanting to get shot. Cody looked at him.

"You pussy, why are you hiding?" Cody demanded.

"Just so you can get shot first," Johnny responded, and they laughed.

Cody sat back on the bed and sucked down as much whiskey as he could. He just stared at the door and waited for it to fly open. As every second ticked by, the tension built. He knew it would only take one cop to shoot one bullet for shit to hit the fan.

Then suddenly, someone smashed the three front glass windows in an attempt to distract them, while at the same time the door flew open. Cop after cop filed in, yelling and pointing their guns. "Down, down. Get the fuck down," they shouted.

Cody just lay on the bed as they cuffed him. They threw Johnny to the floor. By then they both had a very good buzz on. The cops stood them together, and a state cop detective walked up to Cody and held a mug shot up to the side of his head.

"Yep, that's him. We got you Cody. I've been looking for you for months now." He smiled. "I'm glad you didn't shoot us while we were trying to get into the front door." He looked down to the floor. "Where did you guys get all that money from?"

"A supermarket was just hit over in Weymouth for about ninety grand," another cop informed the detective.

The detective, Trooper Harrison from the special state police unit, smiled at Cody and Johnny. "This is my lucky day."

They took Cody and Johnny down to 1010 Commonwealth Ave., the state police headquarters in Boston. It was then that Cody realized that after Jane had dropped them off at the apartment, the cops had arrested her at the end of the street and gotten her to talk about the weapons they had. Once at the station, Trooper Harrison sat Cody down.

"Look, Cody, you're on the run from prison, and one thing I can't understand is why you never left the state or the fucking country. Why stick around here?" he said.

"I wish I knew that answer," Cody told him. "How did you find me?

"It wasn't easy," Harrison said, "but we received word that you were in this section of Boston. So we hit all the local bars. We know you like to drink. We flashed your mug shot around, and people remembered you walking up that one street. Just this morning we started staking out that street. Then out of nowhere, you just pulled up in front of me. I was going to try to take you down when you got out of the car, but I didn't know what kind of gun you had under your coat," he said. "I didn't want a shootout or panic on the streets and bullets flying everywhere, killing some old lady walking by."

Harrison seemed like a straight cop. He had over twenty years in on the force and didn't bust balls. He talked to Cody straight.

"We have a lot to go over, Cody. You know you're going back in to the max joint to finish your time off because you have a life sentence and whatever more the courts give you on top of that," Harrison said. "I'll make this very simple for you. You tell me the shit you did right now from the time you escaped, and I make sure you get nothing added on to your current time. I will have all the gun charges and the robberies run concurrent with your life sentence. All I want to do is clean up these cases. But if I find out you killed anyone out here, we will hang you by your nuts."

Trooper Harrison went on to tell Cody that if they had given him a life sentence and placed him up on a farm with only four years, he would have done the same thing Cody did. "But I would have had some kind of a plan to go somewhere," he said and then laughed.

Cody thought about his offer. "I'll clean up the shit I did, but I won't rat on anyone, and I want Jane and Johnny to walk away from the armed robbery," Cody bargained, trying to make a deal for them.

"No fucking way on your partner Johnny," Harrison shouted. "He was pulling armed robberies with you while he was living at a fucking pre-release center. Give me a break. You should have planned your escape better and gotten out of the country." He paused. "I'll work something out for the girl, Jane, because she's already cooperating with me." He said he would make sure she got probation or something light because she had no record and he wouldn't charge her for harboring a felon or their most recent robbery. But Johnny was looking at least at seven to ten more years.

Cody agreed, and they set dates to go over everything. As Cody and Johnny were escorted out of the state police headquarters, every news media from Boston was outside filming.

Cody and Johnny ate that shit up. The media was making them look like they just got caught off the FBI's ten most wanted list. The press ran the story on the news for days, along with all the major papers. Cody looked over at Johnny and smiled, saying, "I bet anything Danny wishes he was with us right now."

"As sick as that sounds, you're probably right," Johnny replied.

Chapter Fourteen

The commissioner of corrections didn't think it was very funny at all. He took a lot of heat, and a lot of questions were asked, how a lifer was placed up on a prison farm after only serving five years? Also, why was Johnny never accounted for while he was in a pre-release center? It couldn't be proven that he had been out robbing places five days a week with Cody, but they knew he and Cody were both together every day, and they had a strong case against Johnny for the robbery in Weymouth.

The governor had to act quickly. He fired the commissioner and the superintendent of the medium security prison, along with a few guards. Politicians got involved, and they tightened up loose ends. They even removed all of the other lifers off the prison farm and placed them back inside the prison walls.

Fuck 'em, Cody thought. *Fuck 'em. They all should have escaped and they wouldn't have to worry about going back to inside the prison walls.* All of the officials within the correction system were pissed off at Cody and Johnny. Cody knew that once the new administration took over the Corrections Department, everything would quiet down over time. And time was certainly on his side.

Once Cody and Johnny were placed back into the maximum prison, they threw them into the segregation unit—a prison within a prison. It held about twenty-five inmates per tier and about one hundred total. Most of the inmates were there for disciplinary problems within the prison or waiting trial for crimes like murder and assault that had taken place inside the prison.

In segregation, inmates were locked up twenty-three hours

a day and only got out of their cells for one hour a day to take a shower and talk to other inmates. They had plenty to read and drugs were never an issue because certain guards brought them to the prisoners from the friends within the inmate population.

Cody told Johnny about the offer that was on the table from Trooper Harrison. He planned to settle everything from his crime spree since his escape and take Harrison's offer for all the charges to run current with his life sentence. That way Cody didn't have to worry about getting any more time added to his sentence. It would also help get Jane off completely. Johnny would only go down for the armed robbery and a gun charge. Cody always told Johnny the truth, and Johnny respected that. Soon enough, Trooper Harrison pulled Cody out of the prison to go over everything with an attorney.

After the papers were signed, Cody bounced around from court to court, pleading guilty to all of his crimes and getting everything he had agreed to. It was like having a free crime spree on the run and getting no time for it. The judges and district attorney didn't care. They saw Cody was doing life and just went a long with the plea agreement.

Cody was taken to court on the escape charge and received an additional three to five years for escaping from the prison farm. Cody figured it didn't matter. It calculated out to only another nine months extra after he served his fifteen years.

Johnny went to trial and was hit hard with seven to ten years, of which he had to serve at least seven with parole or nine years with no parole. They knew he would never get back into another pre-release program, which gave them something to laugh about.

Cody and Johnny each had to serve roughly eight months in the segregation unit, mainly for the escape charges. It was the Corrections Department's way of letting everything cool down. They both went to court for the charges, and it didn't matter to the prison officials. They still had to face the prison's disciplinary board and disciplinary charges.

When someone was charged with a crime like escape, assault, murder, or drugs in a prison, the prison officials held a hearing to punish them. Cody thought it was funny because they pulled him in front of a board of three people, and it was their job to find him guilty or not guilty of the offence he was accused of committing. And all the three members were guards.

When Cody went before the disciplinary board, the head guard asked him, "How do you plead?"

"Guilty as hell," Cody said.

The guard laughed. "You know Cody, we have a report about an inmate named Richardson who was your roommate down on the farm. He was out on furlough for a weekend, and he told us that he was walking down near the combat zone in Boston. A car drove up on the sidewalk and ran him over. He swears it was you and Johnny."

Cody looked at them and asked, "Did the car kill him?"

He said no.

Cody sat back and smiled. "Well then it couldn't have been me because I would have hit him and then backed up over the fucking rat bastard and made sure he was dead."

Everyone in the room laughed their asses off.

After their stay in the segregation unit, Cody and Johnny were released back to the prison population. They knew they had to start over getting use to the prison bullshit again. The only thing was that this time, people had respect for them because they got one over on the system. The one thing about inmates was they tried very hard each day of their lives to get one over on anyone they could, and they looked up to people who were better at it than them.

As prisoners, they got up each morning not knowing what the day was going to be like inside. They could look the wrong way at another guy and get stabbed before noon. It was a hellish place full of inmates that had every different personality imaginable. Violence was a way of life. There were basic rules most inmates had to learn very quickly in order to survive: don't trust anyone, and if you came in by yourself, only you could get yourself out of prison and not the guy in the next cell you thought was your friend.

Cody and Johnny were lucky to have each other, and Danny was back inside, too. The three had a friendship that was inseparable. But for the inmates that were doing a lot of time, most of those guys had become institutionalized. They got to know everyone, they understood the pain and feelings every new guy felt when he first came through the gates, and they really didn't give a shit what happened to any of them over time. But they did feel for them when they first walked through the gates.

Cody and Johnny hooked up with Danny again. They talked and laughed about the last escape and wished they had gotten the hell out of Massachusetts and done shit in another state. Who knows what would have happened. But for Cody, it had been good to be back on the streets, even for that short time.

Danny told the guys he wished he could have been out there with them, but his goal was to get the fuck out of that maximum security joint and back to the medium security place, which was not hard to do. All he had to do was keep out of shit and keep putting in for transfers. Sooner or later they would send him there because if he wasn't any trouble in the maximum prison, they'd move him right along through the system.

There were three stages of prisons in Massachusetts: a maximum, a couple of medium and ten minimum security prisons. They knew the minimum prison was not in the cards for any of them, but the medium was always a sure pop sooner or later.

Chapter Fifteen

A year passed, and they all kept out of trouble. They received transfers back down to the medium security prison, one at a time. At this time, Cody had served a little over six years and was almost twenty three years old. When he arrived back at the medium prison, the guards were not very pleased with him because most of the guards knew Cody should have never been placed on the minimum security farm in the first place with the small amount of time he'd had under his belt.

Cody knew he would have to watch his back around certain guards and kept a low profile. He suspected that there could be some type of retaliation from some of the guards because their buddies had lost their jobs over his escape. Cody and his partners stayed together and went back to their old workout routine and got high each day.

When they entered the prison yard to walk every day, they noticed a difference from their last time there. Part of the prison wall had fallen down from the vibration of the trains that passed outside of it, and it had been replaced with a fence with razor wire around the top for a quick fix. The prison had to wait for money from the state to rebuild the wall.

Cody noticed a pipe hanging straight out from the top of the wall near the fence. The walls were about thirty feet high and had only two guard towers over in that section of the prison. There was also a twenty-foot fence built around the prison yard, and that wall was about twenty feet from the fence.

Cody told Johnny and Danny that they were all going over that fucking wall.

They laughed. "Yeah right."

"I'm not kidding. We can do this," Cody said.

"How are we going over this fence and then the fence attached to the wall?" Danny asked.

Cody stopped and looked at him. "We are going under the first fence and then scaling the fence attached to the wall."

Right there and then they knew he was serious as cancer. The plan to escape went into motion right there. All they needed was a ride waiting on the other side of the wall after they went over it.

There are two things inmates know about prison guards: most of them hated their jobs and most were drunks. None of them liked to work the guard towers. They weren't allowed to have radios or TVs in there. It was boring and a lot of the time they fell asleep.

Most of the tower guards took newspapers or a *Playboy* up with them and jerked off on their shifts. There were seven other armed guard towers that circled the prison, but Cody figured that even if they saw somebody go over the wall from a long distance, they would have to grab their binoculars first and then their radios and rifles and by that time, he, Johnny, and Danny would be over the wall and gone.

One benefit inmates had was plenty of time to plan anything they wanted. They watched the guards closer than the guards watched them. Cody got a hold of a pair of wire cutters from one of the shops, just a small pair to cut the small loops that held the fence to the poles. Each day when they went out to the yard, they sat beside the section of fence they wanted to go under. They acted like they were just talking and horsing around, and Cody cut one of the lead rings each day so that when they were ready, they could get someone to lift it up for them to go under and then climb over the big fence.

They also planned that if they looked up at the towers one day and the guards were sleeping, they would just go for it without the ride and grab someone out of their car if they had to. They were excited about the plan and didn't give a shit if they got shot off the top of the wall.

All they knew was that they were going to try it soon. As each day went by, they got more hyped. Johnny, who was the fastest of the three of them, wanted to know where would they go and what they would do.

"Let's deal with that shit after we get over the wall and back out in the streets," Cody told him.

Day after day as they walked the yard, they kept checking the fence to see if the guards had found it loose, but they never did. Cody knew the idiot guards were much slower than the maximum prison guards. Everything was so lax there.

They planned to leave on a Sunday morning. Their reasoning was simple: they knew the guards would be hung over and slow. Danny went through some Charlestown guys who were going to drive up and pull over on the side of the road at 7:45 AM. Cody asked Danny if his guy was reliable, and he said it was a sure thing.

Sunday came, and they all dressed in jeans, light jackets and hats. They all made up their beds by putting pillows under the covers. They had gotten hair from the barber shop and glued it to the top of their pillows to make it look like they were still sleeping when the guards made their rounds.

They got out to the yard and it was overcast and misty. There were about twenty inmates out walking, running, or just sitting.

Cody turned to Danny. "Are you sure your connection is reliable and there will be a car there?" he asked again.

"You can count on it, Cody," Danny exclaimed. "I deal with this kid all the time and his brother will be out there waiting for us."

Just then, Cody noticed a kid named Kevin walking with a couple of friends. He yelled over, asking Kevin if he would walk with him because he needed to speak to him. Kevin was a little hesitant at first but agreed. Cody explained to Kevin their plan to go over the wall that morning and asked if he would grab the bottom of the fence so they could crawl under.

"All you have to do is just lift it up and walk away," Cody said.

He told Cody it would be no problem.

They walked another lap around the yard. It was now about 7:40 AM, and they noticed one of the guards in the left tower napping and the other reading a paper, which left only one guard as a potential problem. He would only see them if he looked to his right and took his eyes off the Sunday paper he was reading.

"We go for it on the next lap around," Cody told the guys. "Look for the car, get in it, and have him get the hell out of town."

They reached the loose fence and put on their gloves. Kevin yelled, "Good luck guys," as he lifted up the fence. They got under it fast and made their way over to the wall. All three scaled the fence and got to the top. Johnny was the first over. Holding down that razor wire sucked. It acted like a slinky and started bouncing every which way and cut everybody up. It took the gloves right off Cody's hands as he leaped toward the pipe.

Johnny and Danny flipped over and grabbed the other side of the fence. Cody jumped for the pipe and hung off of it. Then he took a deep breath and let go, dropping thirty feet to the ground. His ass bounced off the tar road on the other side. He heard no gun fire at all. There was another fence twenty yards away with just barbed wire on it. He ran for it and went over without a problem.

Danny was with Cody, but and Johnny was nowhere to be found. They look near the road. No fucking car.

"Where is the fucking car?" Cody yelled to Danny.

"Maybe he's running late," Danny said. "He should be here."

"Are you kidding me, Danny? We can't wait here for him." Cody said.

They were both bleeding from the razor wire. That stuff cut

fast and a person didn't feel it at all. They called out for Johnny as they started running into the woods.

"Did Johnny make it over the wall?" Cody asked.

"Hell yes," Danny said. "He was hauling ass in front on me, and I didn't see what direction he went." As they ran deeper into the woods, he told Cody how the razor wire had ripped his gloves right off his hands.

"Listen," Cody said suddenly, stopping. "Do you hear that??

Danny stopped and listened, too. "What?" he asked. "We did it. If the guards had seen anything, the sirens would be going off, that would let everyone in the area know there has been a prison escape, mostly from the farm."

"We have to get somewhere to steal a car and get some place safe," Cody said.

The blood on their hands made the cuts look worse than they actually were. Small cuts produced a lot of blood. They had no idea where they were. They walked down a small road that had some houses around and started looking into cars for the keys. Someone must have seen them from one of the houses because all of a sudden a couple of cop cars showed up.

"Freeze," the cops yelled.

They took off running back into the woods and ended up in a swamp.

"Shit," Danny said. "We can't get caught now after getting over that prison wall."

"Well if the ride had been there, we would be halfway into Boston by now," Cody snapped.

A few more small town cops showed up with dogs and started looking for them. The damn dogs caught up with them and they were busted. The cops tossed Cody and Danny into a police car and took them to the town police station. They asked why they were both covered in blood and then asked if they were from the prison. They didn't say anything.

The sergeant ordered one of the other officers to call the prison and the prison farm and see if they were missing any inmates.

After an hour, the cop came back and said the prison did a full count and nobody was missing from inside the prison or the prison farm. Cody and Danny glanced at each other, smiling.

By then, the cops were totally confused and wondered why these two guys were all bloody and trying to steal a car. They could not figure out what was going on. Cody and Danny both thought about the dummies in the beds and figured the guards had just looked into the rooms and thought they were sleeping and counted their dummies in place of them.

The sergeant had them transferred to the hospital to get their wounds stitched and then brought them back to process them for trying to steal a car. Cody and Danny gave them phony names for the booking process, and the cops started to think maybe they broke into someone's home and killed somebody.

"The hell with this," the sergeant shouted. "Call that fucking prison again and have them do another count."

Another hour went by and they got another call back stating all inmates were accounted for. But for some reason, the cops were not buying it and asked the prison to send some people down to see if they could identify these two guys. Soon enough, in walked Superintendent Jordan with three guards. He looked at Cody and Danny, who were handcuffed and sitting on a bench.

"Son of a bitch," he said. "Yes, these are our guys, but they were inside the prison walls and not the farm." Superintendent Jordan got on the phone and ordered a full stand up count, which meant every inmate had to be visible and standing outside his doorway. He was afraid he might have a mass escape from inside the prison on his hands.

"How the hell did you guys get out?" he demanded of Cody and Danny. "Do you have a tunnel or what?" Jordan knew what had happened the last time Cody escaped from the prison farm and that the commissioner and the previous superintendent had been fired because of it. He was in a panic.

The prison guards called Jordan back. "Three inmates not accounted for sir," they informed him.

"Lockdown the prison," Superintendent Jordan shouted. He turned to the cop and told him only one other inmate was missing.

The cop's face dropped. "Only one more?" the cop said. "Are you sure this time? You fucking guys get paid for keeping these scum balls locked up behind thirty-foot fucking walls. You can't even do that right!"

By now, they could hear the sirens going off for miles around, warning residents within the town that there had been a prison escape. Cody and Danny smiled at each other and hoped Johnny was far away.

The superintendent glanced over and saw them smiling. He jumped at Cody and got right in his face. "You think this is funny?" he snapped. "This is the second and last time you will ever have this shot again. I'll see to it that you're kept in the maximum joint until you die."

Cody head butted him in the face, breaking his nose, and yelled, "Yeah, maybe so, but I know one thing. You won't be working in Corrections much longer, you son of a bitch."

They tackled Cody to the ground, and Danny started to yell and kick them. They quickly subdued them both.

"Get a van down here to transport these assholes back up to their other home," Superintendent Jordan shouted after he stopped the bleeding from his nose. "I have to call the commissioner."

Chapter Sixteen

"Here we go again," Cody said to Danny in the back of the van as they headed back up to the segregation unit.

"You have to stop getting me in all this shit all the time," Danny laughed."I hope you broke that fucker's nose."

Cody laughed. "It was just a reaction. He came at me so fast, I didn't know what he was going to do, and I had to get the first shot in."

"What do you think about Johnny?" Danny asked.

"Let's hope for the best and see what happens," Cody said but also told Danny that he wished the car had been there.

They arrived at the maximum security prison and were escorted right into the segregation unit.

"Welcome back boys," a guard yelled. "It didn't take you long to find your way back home."

They had already heard about Cody and Danny fighting the superintendent. Fifteen guards surrounded Cody and Danny as they had their chains removed.

"Fucking swing on one of my officers and we will beat you to a fucking pulp," the head guard warned them.

No problem," Cody said. "We have no beef with you."

Off to their cells they went.

Cody couldn't stop thinking about Johnny. *He made it. He's free and soon he will be out there getting laid and drinking up a storm.* The thought of it made Cody very happy, knowing they had all gotten over the wall. Though he hadn't thought of it at the time, it had been one hell of a fall from the top of the wall. He remembered how his ass bounced off the ground. He was lucky he'd fallen the right way or he would be lying there dead because the guards never saw them go over that big fucking wall.

Cody, Danny, and Johnny were the talk of all the prisons in Massachusetts for a while. Everyone thought they had balls, not only to climb over a wall in daylight but also to get over fourteen guards fired along with that asshole superintendent. Cody knew he would be in the maximum prison for the long haul now, and he was buried in the segregation unit for a while. The days were very long in segregation. Being locked in an eight-by-ten-foot cell with only books for twenty-three hours a day could play with a man's mind. But the one thing they couldn't take from him was is his thoughts and dreams.

Three weeks after the escape, the police caught Johnny over in Boston. They placed him in a cell near Cody.

"How did they catch you? Cody asked Johnny.

"After I got over the wall, I didn't see a car and just kept running," Johnny said. "I thought you guys were behind me." He had followed the train tracks and then hopped aboard a train. The train took him into Boston. He'd had nowhere to go and no money. The lucky bastard hadn't even gotten cut up on the razor wire.

He told Cody nobody was around Boston anymore. Everybody they knew was in prison. Cody told Johnny what had happened with him and Danny and that he wanted to get the bastard who never showed up with the car. Even though Johnny had been caught, his excitement about their accomplishment of going over the prison wall and making it shined in his eyes.

"Sit back, my friend," Cody said to him. "We will soon be out in the prison population, but I believe we are going to here for a while."

They were in the segregation for about six months before they were released back into the prison population once again. They had each received another three to five years added onto their sentences for their escape, but receiving more time didn't matter to any of them because they knew the prison system and how to play the game. They had come to terms with their situations and started to lose hope of ever getting out again. They were prepared to die in prison if they had to. But at least they were together and had each others back. They were grateful for that.

Cody made the best of his situation. He confided in Johnny that he didn't want to just sit back and do his time. He suggested they should gain their own power within the prison. The one thing both Cody and Johnny had going for them was that the other older inmates didn't have was a strong bond with Danny and their friends from way back in the juvenile centers.

They were a new generation of inmates that the old-time inmates were not used to dealing with. The young inmates only believed in drugs. Cody knew this and used it to his advantage. Most of the young inmates respected Cody and Johnny because of what they had each done during their time being locked up.

The older inmates believed in all of their respect and feared the older gangsters that had run everything within the prison population for years. The gangsters had control over all the drugs in the prison, ran the booking, and took all the other inmates' money. They used guys like Cody when he first came there and made him feel like part of their group, but in reality they only used him. Cody and his associates from as far back as the youth centers believed the gangsters' respect shit was overrated.

Cody took advantage of it. He gathered all the guys he met in the Department of Youth Services and brought all them together to create one large operation. Cody acquired people from Southie, Charlestown, Cambridge, Dorchester, and Hyde Park. He explained to them how he thought the prison should be run and his vision. He went on and explained all of the benefits they would reap being a strong controlled force.

No matter what, Johnny and Danny always had Cody's back. They let him call the shots, just as he had on the streets. Cody knew if they could control the drugs in the prison, they would control everything, which would bring even more people over to their side. They also wanted all the booking operations. That way, his group could reap all the benefits.

To get everything going, Cody group's had to make a stand. They needed to move swiftly and aggressively against the older gangsters. Everybody knew Frankie ran the show, but now it was Cody and his associate's time to take over. Cody and his friends had to come up with a strategy once and for all. They were going to take everything away from those mob guys while at the same time, turn the prison around in their favor by making a statement that would shock the inmates and the prison administration. Cody would then have the power and his group would have everything they wanted.

Chapter Seventeen

The prison officials didn't want to take drugs out of the prison system because it helped control the inmates and keep a balance over how they lived. Everybody knew how most of the drugs came into the prison. Girlfriends or wives would visit and bring balloons filled with drugs. An inmate would swallow the balloons one at a time and then go back to his room and either try to throw them up or crap them out the next day.

An inmate that wanted to get an ounce of pot into the prison would pack a condom full of pot and then slide it up his well-greased ass. Then when he returned to his cell, he would sit on his toilet and shit it out.

The majority of inmates just received cash to support their habits. Most of the wise guys received a third of all the large drugs that came into the prison, plus they had guards and other prison staff members bring in drugs. Drugs were worth tons of money in prison, and whoever had the most ran everything. A joint cost five bucks, and a bag of heroin was fifty dollars. Downers, uppers, or whatever—any inmate could buy any kind of drug they wanted in the prison system. They could also negotiate and have anyone killed for any kind of drugs.

Cody knew the fucking junkies would sell their souls for a bag of dope or a couple of pills. Cody had never stuck a needle in his arm and always just smoked pot or took a valium once in a while to relax. He never liked letting his guard down and never wanted drugs to control him. And after watching guys on the streets shoot drugs, he knew what the outcome would be.

It was around 8:00 PM on a Friday night when Danny, who

had just started shooting drugs, found out one of the older gangsters had a large amount of drugs coming in through the visiting room. He found out one of their flunkeys, whose name was Louie, was getting it past the guards. Johnny and Cody came up with a plan. They would go to the Louie's room and convince him to throw up the balloons. They would take the drugs and deal with Frankie and the bullshit the next day.

So when Louie got back to his cell on the third floor of his block, Cody, Danny, and Johnny walked right in behind him catching Louie off guard.

"You have two minutes to toss up those balloons or we will kill you and cut them out of you," Cody told Louie.

"You know whose drugs these are," Louie said to them. "If you fuck with me, you will all be dead by morning." He pushed Cody. "Go fuck yourselves!"

Johnny grabbed the motherfucker by the neck and started to strangle him. Louie tried to kick, but Danny grabbed his feet and held on tight. Cody took out his knife and aimed it toward Louie's eyeball.

"Are you going to cooperate with us?" Cody asked.

Louie tried to spit in Cody's face, and Cody pushed the knife deep into Louie's eye socket and straight into whatever brains the guy had. Louie's body went limp instantly.

"Shit," Danny said in a panic. "He's fucking dead. This wasn't the plan. Now what?"

Cody told him to calm down. "Let's get what we came for." He quickly pulled the knife from Louie's eye and ran it in and out of his stomach several times, making a hole. Johnny stuck his gloved hand into Louie's stomach and pulled out the balloons. He put them in the cell's sink to wash off the blood.

"Did you get all of them?" Danny asked.

Johnny looked up at him. "How the fuck do I know? I think we have enough."

They washed the blood off of the balloons, took off their

gloves, and walked out of the room one at a time, trying not to draw any attention to themselves.

They hid the drugs well, and before 10:00 PM, word traveled throughout the prison that its first murder of the year had occurred. Each time there was a murder, the prison locked down the block and called in the state police in to investigate. And after that, it was business as usual. The prison officials liked to have the prison back up and running in a day or two. Nobody had seen anything, and Cody was sure they found some more drugs in the fucker's body. He figured the officials and state police more than likely thought some junkies killed Louie.

Once the block opened again, they counted forty balloons Johnny had pulled out of Louie's body. It was a great score, all heroin and pills. Cody passed the drugs out to his group and told everyone to start selling the stuff.

"Let's pull in some money," Cody said. "And make sure if some people don't have money now, let them owe us."

"What the hell?" Danny said. "Nobody deals like that in prison."

"We will because if they don't come up with our money, they will owe us a favor or we can send them down to Johnny for a loan. Then we can get back a few dollars more or even better or they will get hurt," Cody said.

The drugs initially belonged to the Italians, and word traveled quickly down to them. Frankie was in charge. He knew Cody, Danny, and Johnny hadn't only killed their guy, but that they'd done it viciously. Frankie thought maybe Cody didn't understand who the drugs belonged to, so he set up a meeting with the three of them in the prison yard.

Cody and Johnny had about forty inmates hang out in the yard when they met with Frankie and instructed everyone to take Frankie's entire group out if something went down. Frankie walked up to Cody, swinging his hands and all that Italian bullshit, asking if he knew about the drugs going around the prison.

Cody looked Frankie right in the eye and said "Fuck you.

You're done here. You guys are not running shit anymore. We're taking over, and if you get in our fucking way, you will never leave this place alive."

"Do you know what you're getting yourself into, Cody? It don't have to be this way. You give us the drugs back and we can work together," Frankie yelled.

"Like that would ever happen," Cody shouted and then turned to walk away. But he stopped, turned around, and got back in Frankie's face again. "You know what, Frankie, you piece of shit? It does have to be this way. Look around you. You have ten guys here with you. I got an army around me, and we will take you out right here where you stand you fat fuck! Starting today, we are going to take over this place, and you will not have anymore say on what is going to happen in this prison. As a matter of fact, I believe you should start giving us half of everything you bring in."

Frankie was appalled. He shouted, "You young kids have no respect for anything or anyone." In that moment, he looked bad in front of his crew. He'd never had anyone speak to him like that before. Everybody had always kissed his and his crew's asses for years in the joint.

"Say another word to me and I'll kill you right where you stand," Cody threatened. Frankie didn't say a word. "I thought so, you ball-less bastard." He turned once again and walked away with Johnny and Danny by his side.

Danny and Johnny could not believe what Cody had just told Frankie.

"Where the hell did that all come from?" Danny said. "That wasn't the plan. I didn't know you were going to say all that shit."

Johnny just laughed. "I loved the look on that gangster's face. He has never been spoken to like that before. He looked like he was going to shit himself when you told him you would kill him right there were he stood."

Cody smiled and felt a real power overcome him. He reveled in how great it made him feel. He had taken a stand that day.

Why should he and his partners take a back seat for anything in this fucking prison? They lived here and had more on the ball than those wise guys ever did.

"Fuck them," Cody said. "From today on, we want part of every drug or anything else that comes into this place. And if they don't like it, we will send them out in body bags."

Danny was afraid Cody was getting a little psycho, but he and Johnny were down for anything and liked the way Cody took control of everything. Cody didn't just make a plan, but he could change the plan at any given moment and follow through with it to the very end. Cody and his group of friends had learned an old saying from the street: keep your friends close but your enemies closer. In prison, the saying was a little different: keep your friends close and kill anyone who gets in your way.

Cody and his partners started booking bets down in their end of the prison and sold drugs. They now had about fifty guys in their group and were growing fast. But Frankie wasn't backing down that easily. He hadn't taken or understood Cody's warning out in the yard seriously.

Frankie didn't know the extent to which Cody would go. He was not an everyday inmate. Cody spoke with his partners and about fifteen other guys he trusted. He explained to everyone that they needed to put some fear into Frankie and show his small gang and all the other Italians they were not fucking around anymore. "We call the shots around here now," Cody said.

Cody asked everyone for their ideas on how to deal with the situation. Cody was smart in that way. He knew the way he wanted things done, but he never came out in a group and demanded this or that. He always spoke in a normal, quiet voice and then sat back. He had open conversations with his peers. He let everybody speak and listened to what people were saying. He would jump in as soon as someone started talking about the way Cody wanted the job done and get everybody to agree on it. That way, he made it seem like he used their ideas and they all felt great about it.

Chapter Eighteen

They came up with a plan and agreed if they killed Frankie, his crew would back down and run around like chickens with their heads cut off. Frankie was a mafia guy, but Cody and his friends didn't give a crap. That gangster stuff was big on the streets back in the day, but Cody and his friends were changing the rules and making the prison their house. Everyone knew it was a big challenge to take out a mob guy, but everyone like the idea of starting at the top and pushing the fat fuck off his throne.

They were going to send a statement to all of the gangsters on the streets about who was running the prison from that moment on and that if any of Cody's associates' families got fucked with, other Mafia guys in prison would die. The gangsters would realize if they got caught out on the streets, they would have to go through the maximum security prison themselves someday.

For some reason, all of the Italians went to the prison's church every Sunday and then hung there for an hour and drank coffee with the priest before they went on with their days. On Sundays, Cody and Johnny got high and laughed at them. They could never understand how the gangsters could try to be so religious on Sundays and go right out and kill people and pull crimes all week long until the next Sunday rolled around.

Cody and Johnny looked at the Italians' Sunday routine as an advantage in their favor because if they wanted to get all of them at once, they could do it in the church on Sunday morning and let them all rest in peace. So, they planned to take out Frankie on an early Sunday morning.

Putting their plan in motion, Cody and his two partners

decided to go to church the following Sunday and make a point of being noticed by the priest. The priest would be their star witness for their alibi. The plan was to make Frankie uncomfortable and get him to leave the prison church before Cody and his partners. They would then have three guys waiting in the block to nail Frankie when he returned.

Cody and the guys sat through the service. Afterward, they walked up and started bullshitting with the Italian priest, asking him when they were going to get an Irish priest in there. As they sat down to have coffee, Frankie must have felt like something was wrong. He got the hell out of there. He walked into his block, passed the guard in the hall, and headed toward his room. As he entered his cell, they grabbed him from out of nowhere. Stab, stab, stab. They stabbed him three times in the throat. Frankie tried to yell but couldn't. He panicked and tried to run. They followed after him. Another guy knifed him in the back. Stab, stab, stab. He went down. They stabbed him ten more times in his throat to make sure he drowned in his own blood.

Back in the prison church, Cody and the boys were still there when a guard ran in, yelling, "Prison lockdown. Prison lockdown."

Cody, Danny, and Johnny made sure the priest looked at each of them.

"Say a pray for us father," they said. "See you next week."

"Please make it a point to return here next Sunday," the priest called after them.

Cody walked out of the church beside one of Frankie's crew members. He turned toward the guy. "I hope that fat fucking boss of yours didn't have an accident."

The guy just looked at him. Cody smiled and walked back to his block.

Just as they thought it would, word spread quickly again. Another murder, the second of the year, and it wasn't just anybody. It was Frankie, the big Mafia guy that had been running the place for years. The prison officials had no idea there was a power struggle going on within the prison and figured it could have been a hit from the streets. They lugged half of Frankie's crew to segregation and kept the others locked up in their cells in case more shit went down in retaliation.

They brought in the organized crime unit from the state police force, fearing Frankie's murder could result in a war on the streets. Nobody just kills a wise guy, after all. He had been a key guy in the Boston mob. Cody knew Frankie had to have told somebody about their altercation in the prison yard. He had a feeling he would somehow be brought into the mix by some of the rat bastard gangsters on the streets or even his friends inside.

Sure enough, the investigation of Frankie's murder started, and they called half of Cody's group down. Cody and his partners had the greatest alibi around—their time with the priest. The investigators asked Cody about Frankie's murder, and Cody explained he had been at church at the time and knew nothing about it. They sent him back to his cell. It was way too easy. Cody and his friends knew all they had to do now was lay back and wait. The officials would never be able to prove Cody and his partners killed Frankie.

The prison stayed on lockdown for about a week. After they opened it back up, Cody learned about fifteen of Frankie's crew had been taken out of the maximum security prison and transferred to the other two medium security prisons because some claimed they feared for their lives. *What a bunch of bullshit. They were all just lost without their fat ass leader*, Cody thought.

Cody let everything cool down for about a month before he started up the drugs and booking once again. By now, everybody knew one group was running things and not just one person. Most inmates didn't care who ran things. They just needed to know who to deal with for a bet on a game and, more importantly, where to get their daily drugs to support their habits.

Cody and his group made sure that if anyone had drugs brought inside the prison, his group received half of everything. Cody had one demand from everyone in their group: that all inmates in the segregation unit would be supplied with anything they needed, drugs, cigarettes, soap and candy, all the time at no charge. Cody knew what it was like to be locked up twenty-three hours a day. Anyone was released from the segregation unit came out with big respect for Cody and his friends and joined up with them as soon as they were back out in general population.

They got word in from the streets through a few Charlestown and Southie guys that the North End guys were not happy with what happened to Frankie. They were demanding to know who wacked him. Cody sent word over to Southie to tell those North End guys that half the fucking prison had something to do with it and that they'd better not act up or their other pals in the prison system would get it, too. They never heard back from the North Enders. They wrote Frankie off like nothing had ever happened, and it stayed a dead issue.

Chapter Nineteen

Cody and his group had to find other avenues to get different items into the prison. They knew Frankie and his crew had guards and other people in their back pockets. Cody was on a mission. He had to find the guards, medics, or instructors that wanted to earn extra money.

He and his partners put word out into the population. There would be a big payoff for anyone who came to Cody with information on who could be bought. The first idea was to go look at some of the instructors. The instructors were not guards. They were outside tradesmen that taught inmates skills in metal or woodworking within the prison. The prison had a wood shop and two metal shops for the production of license plates and sewer covers for the state.

Late one afternoon, Cody and Johnny received word that there was an instructor named Tony who ran the license plate shop. He made extra money off of inmates by bringing them burgers and other food from the street. It made sense. Inmates would die for outside food, and the instructor couldn't be charged for bringing contraband into the prison.

So, Cody and a Johnny approached the guy and asked if he would bring them a couple of grinders and asked how much it would cost.

The guy smiled. "Well if you could come up with twenty, I'll get them for you."

Cody reached into his pocket, handed him the money, and told the guy he would see him tomorrow. The next day, Cody and Johnny went to see Tony to pick up their grinders. Cody handed the guy another fifty.

"What's this for?" Tony asked.

"It's a tip for you," Cody said.

As they turned to walk away, Tony said just what Cody wanted to hear: "If you need more, just let me know."

Cody turned around and walked back to Tony. He pulled out a couple of grand, all in hundred dollar bills. Tony stared at the money.

"I could have you busted for having that kind of money in here," he said.

"Yes, you could," Cody said, "but you won't because I make money like this all the time in here. If you want to make some real money and stop fucking around bringing fast food shit in, bring me in what I want."

Then Tony started to ask a lot of questions, which was great because Cody knew he had Tony right where he wanted him. Otherwise Tony would have just said he was not interested.

"I need drugs," Cody stated.

"I don't know how to get drugs on the street," Tony protested.

"Look Tony, this is how easy it is," Cody explained. "We will have someone meet you anywhere you want. They'll give you a package once a week, you bring it in to me or Johnny, and we will give you a grand a week in cash. That would be four thousand dollars a month for you and your family and close to fifty grand a year. How easy is that?"

Tony thought about it for a moment. "What about me getting searched every day coming in here?"

"You know how they search you. Stick the package up your ass for all I care. Your job is to get the package in to me and nobody will know anything. You will be making triple the money from me than what the state pays you." He again reminded Tony it would all be in cash.

"One other thing," Cody told Tony. "Don't ever open any of

the packages. Just bring whatever it is in to me, and we will get along fine and there will be no problems."

Tony agreed and gave Cody his home phone number so someone could contact him. The following week, Tony started to bring in the packages. It cost them a lot more than they wanted to pay, but they were able to get a lot more drugs and a better variety.

Not long after that, a Charlestown guy who hung with Cody mentioned he had a brother who owned a used car dealership. He asked if they could get a hold of some dealer plates. He offered Cody five hundred per plate.

"Of course we can," Cody said with a big smile. "After all, the inmates make all the license plates for the whole goddamn state of Massachusetts right here in this prison." And they had Tony, who ran the whole shop, on their payroll.

Getting dealer plates would not only be easy, but getting them out would be even easier. The guards never checked visitors or staff for anything going out of the prison, only coming in. So they flooded the streets with dealer plates and got five bills a plate. If dealers had to pay the state for the plate, it cost them more than two thousand dollars. Buying from Cody was a better deal.

Cody had Tony take out five sets a week and kicked him one hundred per set. Tony was happy as a pig in shit to be making all of that money. He wasn't that bright either. Over time, Cody had people from the street dealing and doing all sorts of shit right from Tony's house.

But no matter how great thing were running inside and even though Cody and his partners were making plenty of money, it never seemed to be good enough. Cody wasn't doing it for the money. He was in prison and had no use for money at all. He sent most of his share out to his mom and all she did was play the lottery and go to bingo. All Cody wanted to do was get one over on the system and see how far he could push any situation, no matter the consequences. It was a game for Cody.

He started to lose it. He now had about eight years in, and every day he watched inmates he knew leave one at a time and then return again later because they got into more shit. Johnny said he understood why inmates liked returning to prison. In prison they had no responsibilities. There were no bills to pay, free medical, free dental, and a room and three meals a day. How good was that? The only worry they had each day was to find their high.

By that time, Danny was turning into a junkie and had Johnny shooting drugs with him. Cody was not happy about it at all. He liked Danny, but he still remembered how he'd messed up the escape and how he had gotten all bent out of shape when they took out Louie. Cody always kept in mind that he had grown up with Johnny and that Danny was with him only because Johnny brought him in. But deep down, Cody loved those two guys, who had stayed by his side like brothers.

Chapter Twenty

One day, they were sitting on the flats playing cards and messing around when Johnny, stoned out of his mind, said, "I'm really bored as hell and we need to wake this place up a little."

"What do you have in mind?" Cody asked.

"Let's get this place going and set the three barrels on fire and rip this block apart tonight!" Johnny exclaimed.

"Great idea," Danny said.

They put word out in the block that they were going to start some shit around 10:00 PM, right before lockup. That night, the guard yelled, "Time for lockup. All inmates return to your cells."

At that moment, Danny threw a plastic mop bucket down from the third tier. It landed right on the guard's head, hitting him dead on the money. The guard dropped like a rock and hit the floor. Everyone started to set fires and threw trash everywhere. Over sixty inmates participated, all of them just letting off steam.

Other guards came running down to the block and saw one of their fellow officers was down. They tried to rush into the block and pull him out, but the inmates started fighting them. They picked one guard up and threw him into a flaming trash barrel. Guards with shotguns that fired rubber bullets came in, and everybody ducked and hid. Next, they fired in gas. The inmates were choking, but nobody gave a shit.

"Send in some more motherfuckers," the prisoners screamed, and they did.

The guards were finally able to get everything under control and started lugging inmates to segregation. Cody, Danny, and Johnny were the first to go. The guards, dressed in riot gear, kicked their asses all the way up to the segregation unit. The small disturbance in the block rejuvenated Cody and his partners. They hadn't felt that alive since going over the wall. Things like that woke them up and helped the inmates release stress and tension and blow off steam.

While they were in the segregation unit, Cody spoke with Danny and Johnny about how fucking bored he still was and how he needed a new way to vent and get on with his time. Maybe he would break out again. They laughed.

"What the hell are you talking about Cody?" they asked. "Go do some drugs or something. Go get yourself high. You know you're never leaving this prison. There is nothing out on the streets for any of us anymore. Everyone we all know is either dead or in prison with us."

They did just about everything they could do in that prison. They got everything they needed and did whatever the hell they wanted. Danny and Johnny thought Cody was losing it with his talk about getting out on the streets again. They paid no attention to him.

Cody shook his head in disgust and went back to his cell, knowing they didn't understand. They just didn't fucking get it. Cody was trying to reach out to them, hoping they would come up with some ideas to help him with his thought process. But no, they couldn't care less. Cody understood in that moment that his partners now only thought about getting high and not getting back outside. He realized then, just as he was starting to lose it, they had already lost it.

He lay in his cell thinking how institutionalized his partners had become. They were dependent on drugs. Cody was pissed at Danny for turning Johnny on to shooting up. When it came to making any kind of decision, it was up to him. They would just follow like fucking puppy dogs.

Chapter Twenty-One

Cody still had another month to serve in the segregation unit. One day when he was out of lockup for his hour and taking a shower, he heard an inmate crying in his cell. Cody walked up and saw a young kid he remembered seeing a couple of times back in his block. The kid was about nineteen and had only been in for two years.

"What's wrong?" Cody asked.

"I can't do it anymore," the kid said. "I'm thinking about killing myself. I have seven more years to do, and I don't know what else I can do."

Their conversation had bad timing for Cody because he was feeling down with his own problems. He had come into the prison at the kid's age and understood how confused he was. But in prison, saying you wanted to kill yourself was a sign of weakness. Normally Cody would have told anybody who wanted to hang themselves to go for it and watch them do it, but there was something about this young kid. Maybe Cody saw a little bit of himself in the kid, something from the time when he himself walked into that hellhole of a prison and being so young in a messed up system. He started to talk with the kid very quietly because, for reasons he didn't understand, Cody wanted learn more about him.

"I've done about eight years," Cody told the kid. "If you go and kill yourself, you will let the system win. Sit back and relax. You can kill yourself anytime. Why do it today?"

The kid smiled. Cody continued, "I'll tell you what. When you get out of this fucking unit, you come and hang with me and my friends and we will help you out. Nobody will ever bother you either."

The kid calmed down because Cody had given him a little hope. Cody lit up a joint and passed it to him. "What is your name and when do you get out of this segregation unit?"

I'm Sean," the kid said, "and I get out in about three weeks."

"Great," Cody said. "When you get out in population, look up this guy named Ramon. I'll also get word out to some other people for them to look after you, Sean. You will be safe, but never talk about killing yourself again, okay?

Sean nodded his head in agreement.

After that, Cody and Sean talked and smoked pot when they got out for their hour each day, and the few weeks went by quickly. Cody found out Sean had killed his father with a golf club while he was sleeping. He killed him because he beat up Sean's mom every time he came home drunk. The courts convicted him of manslaughter, which carried a nine- to twelve-year sentence. He could walk out of prison a free man in nine years with no parole.

The kid liked to smoke a little pot and didn't shoot drugs. Cody started to get attached to him. He liked the kid a lot. He was like a breath of fresh air for Cody. The kid was different. He came from a small town in Massachusetts and didn't know anyone. He wasn't even a criminal. Cody knew he didn't belong in a maximum security prison.

Sean told Cody the only reason he was in the segregation unit was because of the riot. The guards had grabbed him for no reason. Cody just smiled. He understood. He told Sean that he could get into a medium or even a minimum prison within six months and get back out on the streets and be with his family again within six years.

Sean thanked him for everything and admitted he had been very scared to come to prison. Cody told him everybody got scared. "That's what's wrong with the system. You're a young kid who doesn't know anyone, and they put you out into a population where a third of the guys want to make you their bitch or prey upon you because you're weak or alone. The administration doesn't do anything to help a kid like you."

Cody and his partners spent a total of four months in the segregation unit for their little disturbance. After that, they were put back out into population, in the same block as always. The administration figured they would keep a better eye on them if they kept them together. Cody was bummed that Sean wasn't transferred into his block because he couldn't keep an eye on him, but he did get to see him each day at lunch and in the prison yard where they walked around and bullshitted.

Cody knew inmates in every block and had Ramon from Sean's block look after him. Danny and Johnny had their noses out of joint about Sean, but Cody had taken a liking to the kid and took him under his wing. It made him feel good talking with him and teaching him the ways of prison life. Cody showed him the dos and don'ts, what to look for when trouble happened, and how not to get involved in shit that didn't concern him.

Some of the guys couldn't understand what Cody was thinking when they noticed him bonding very fast Sean. One day, they were all sitting around a table, playing cards on the flats in the block.

"Do you mind if I ask you a question in front of everyone?" Danny asked Cody out of nowhere.

"Sure, what's on your mind?" Cody said.

Danny paused a moment and then asked, "What's up between you and this kid Sean?"

"What business is it of yours?" Cody said.

Everyone fell quiet as the card game continued, but Danny pushed the issue.

"You got very close to this kid very quickly," Danny said. "I was just wondering if you wanted to fuck this kid. Don't take this the wrong way, Cody, but you don't even know this kid and you're with him all the time."

Cody looked at Danny with a crazy look in his eyes. He lost

it and nailed Danny right in the jaw. Danny flew back almost three feet and landed on the floor. Johnny and the guys grabbed Cody.

"What are you, going fucking psycho or what?" Danny shouted.

"You would never understand," Cody yelled. "Go stick another fucking needle in your arm, you fucking junkie. You want to play games with me, Danny, do you?"

Johnny let Cody go. Cody turned to face everyone there. "Anyone else here have a problem about Sean or any other sick questions for me? Let me make this very clear to everybody. Sean is with us and God help anyone who fucks with him in this prison."

There were no more words to say after that. Danny knew he'd messed up and didn't know why he would say something so stupid to Cody. He knew Cody wasn't like that. Cody and his friends never let inmates rape other inmates or mess around like that.

"You okay?" Johnny asked Danny.

"Yeah," he said. "I'll be fine."

"Don't ever be that stupid again," Johnny said.

They all had plenty of smut books, and even if they had to jerk off ten times a day, none of Cody's friends ever messed around with another guy. Cody hated gays worse than blacks. He had never forgotten the time the blacks checked him out when he first came to prison. Hell, everybody knew Cody had killed a man for calling him a faggot in front of his girlfriend.

Prison time was getting to everyone. Over the past couple of years everybody had started to change for the worst. Over the next few days, Cody and Danny put things behind them and went on like it had never happened. Everybody knew Cody was not acting like himself. He was always on edge, and with the exception of Sean, nobody understood how he felt or what was running through his mind.

Cody confided in the young kid. Even though he didn't really know him very well, Cody felt at peace with himself when he was with Sean. He loved to listen to the new stories the kid told him about the streets. Sean talked about where he came from and what he had done with his family growing up. Sean liked and listened to Cody's stories as well.

Cody was always in a better mood coming in from the prison yard after talking with Sean. One of the dreams they both laughed and joked about was talking about the days ahead when they would both be free again. They would get out around the same time.

Sean joked he would hook Cody up with his sister and how it would be if Cody became his brother-in-law. They would look back on all of the prison bullshit and be done with it. They both knew it was only dreams, but for now it helped pass the time and let them escape reality.

Chapter Twenty-Two

Cody knew he couldn't let drugs get in his way. Ninety percent of the prison's population was fucked up on some kind of drug every day of the week. He used to see guys blow out every vein in their body shooting up dope. Some guys were shooting up drugs five times a day. Cody understood why everybody was high all the time. It helped them escape reality. But none of the inmates understood anything. They didn't realize the drugs controlled each and every one of them. Cody just collected money off of them day in and day out.

Cody didn't get many visitors. Every now and then other inmate friends of his would set him up with visits from girls they knew from the streets. One day, Cody went to the visiting room with the Ramon. He had his girl bring her friend up to meet Cody. They sat in the visiting room and held hands like kids on their first date.

Cody always felt good after getting a visit, seeing a girl, listening to her soft spoken voice, and touching her soft skin after so many years. Cody didn't mind getting those kind of visits at all because they made him feel great for weeks at a time. He and the girl would just make small talk while cuddling side-by-side in two chairs. Sometime the girls would ask why he was in prison, but Cody never told them. He knew he would probably never see them again, but most of the girls he met wrote to him sometimes, and he always wrote back.

Just when he and the girl Ramon's girlfriend brought along were getting all hot, three guards came into the visiting room out of nowhere and announced visits were over and the prison was going into lockdown. *Shit*, Cody thought. *Why did something have to happen now?* He and the girl kissed and said their good-byes. Cody told her he would write her, and she agreed to write back.

He thanked Ramon for setting up the visit and walked back to his block, wondering what was going on. He soon found out the prison had another murder in one of the blocks. Cody thought nothing of it because it was not in his block and not in the yard. They couldn't question him about it because he had been on a visit.

Cody returned to his cell and lay back on his bed for a couple of hours, thinking about the hot chick that had just visited him. He started writing her a letter, telling her he would like to see her again and that he was sorry the visit was so short. Then out of nowhere, Cody's cell door swung open and three guards ordered Cody to stand up and follow them to the deputy's office.

"What's going on?" Danny and Johnny yelled from their cells.

"I don't know," Cody called back. They had no cuffs on him, so he knew he was not going to segregation.

They escorted Cody down to the deputy superintendent's office. The state police were there.

"Hey, whatever happens, I was on a visit," Cody joked, "and I don't know anything."

They ordered Cody to take a seat. Without saying a word, they stared at Cody as if they were trying to get a reaction out of him. Cody looked at everyone in the office.

"What am I here for?" he asked the deputy.

The state trooper spoke up. "Do you know an inmate by the name of Sean O'Connor?" he asked Cody.

Cody smiled. "You know I do. He's a good kid and a friend of mine, why?"

Again, they looked at Cody for a few moments before speaking. Then they said they had found him dead in his cell earlier that day. Someone strangled him to death. Cody took a deep breath. He was in shock. He shook his head in disbelief.

"No fucking way," he said and then shot to his feet so fast his chair tipped over. "No fucking way."

Cody felt a sadness build up inside of him. He started to yell. "Why didn't you get this young kid out of this shithole? You let this happen to him!" He started to flip out, but Cody knew he could never break down in front of the guards.

They returned him to his and cell and kept the block locked down.

"What happened?" Danny and Johnny yelled down to Cody.

Cody didn't say a word. For the first time in his life, his eyes welled up. He put a pillow over his face so no one could hear and cried into it. He thought about Sean and wondered what he had been thinking during the last seconds of his life. Cody thought Sean had probably been thinking about him and how Cody had told him nobody would ever mess with him. But someone had. Cody's sadness quickly turned into anger. He swore everybody was going to pay for Sean's murder—the fucking people who did it, and the administration that kept the young kid in the maximum security prison, and God Almighty himself.

Danny knew something was up and kept pleading with Cody to say something. After an hour or so, Cody said in a very low and quiet voice, "It's Sean."

"What about Sean?" Danny asked. "Did he get lugged to segregation, caught with drugs, knock out a fucking guard?" he tried to joke and made everybody laugh.

Cody ran to the cell bars in a rage. "Someone fucking killed him over in block eight," he shouted. "They picked him up and strangled the life out of him and killed my little friend Sean."

Silence fell over the whole block.

"You alright, partner?" Johnny called over to Cody.

Cody didn't say a word. He was overcome with sadness. He had just lost the only person who had meant anything to him in prison. Sean had helped him regain a little bit of his sanity each day by talking and laughing in the prison yard and giving Cody stories of hope to get him through another day.

The block remained silent until they reopened the prison the next day. When the cells opened, Danny and Johnny ran over to Cody. They looked into his eyes and knew nothing had to be said. No matter what it took, people were going to pay for the young kid's death at all costs. No one had been taken to the segregation unit for Sean's murder, and that meant the inmates that did it were either trying to send Cody a message or they were just fucking stupid.

Word went out quickly. Drugs, money, or anything people wanted in return for information on the inmates that killed the kid. Everybody asked questions for their own reasons. Some wanted to be the first with the information to get in closer with Cody and his group, others just wanted to see some more shit happen for their own excitement.

Cody and his partners knew they had to use their heads and stay calm. If they did anything too fast or made the wrong move, everything they had built in the prison would be gone and they would all end up with life sentences hanging over their heads. They wanted to get the right person or people.

They figured it had to be more than one guy in the block because that was how it worked in prison. When an inmate wanted to kill somebody, he always needed a lookout or someone to hold down the guy he was going to take out. If just one guy tried to kill someone, there would be a lot of noise and screaming, and the guard in the block would hear the scuffle and observe everything until help arrived.

Cody really hurt as the days went by. He grieved Sean's death. He knew that was what happened when he let himself get attached to people, and he realized he would feel the same if something happened to Danny or Johnny. He realized everybody he came into contact with either died or got hurt. It was a violent prison world he lived in. It was worse than the streets. Just when he thought he had control over things, the unexpected always seemed to happen.

Chapter Twenty-Three

After two months, Cody and everybody in his group started to lose all hope of finding Sean's killers. They really wanted someone to pay for what happened and looked for the smallest bit of information. Finally, Ramon received word that Sean had a small altercation in block eight shortly before he was killed. Sean had seen three guys muscling another inmate for drugs that day. Cody guessed Sean had walked by their cell, looked in by mistake, and saw them beating up the other inmate. One of them probably asked Sean what the fuck he was looking at and Sean probably mouthed off to him. Sean knew Cody and his friends had his back.

Cody had tried to school Sean about prison life. He told him every day about other inmates. "If something happens, just keep walking. It doesn't involve you," he had told him time and time again. "If somebody gives you shit, let me or one of our friends know right away." If only he could have had Sean moved into his block or if the prison had transferred him to another institution, he would have still been alive.

Nobody knew much about the inmates that killed Sean. Ramon found out they ran with a small group of ten or fifteen guys and were spread throughout the joint. They were low key guys that shot up four times a day and where nothing but dope heads for the most part.

All Cody could think about was how those tough guys preyed upon that weak kid, taken advantage of the situation, and killed his young friend. Everyone agreed the killers would pay with their lives. Cody and Ramon gathered their group together in the prison yard, choosing only the psychopaths and sociopaths. Cody himself had been diagnosed with a sociopath disorder by the prison psychologist many years before.

Everyone in the group knew they could always count on Cody for anything, and Cody knew he could count on them. He and Ramon explained the situation and spoke about Sean, about how the fucking system let the young kid down, and about how those assholes killed him for no reason. Cody told them Sean's death not only had to be revenge out of loyalty, but that they were going put fear into the prison so nobody would ever fuck with another member of their group ever again.

They came up with a plan to set up groups of two to three of their most trusted friends and have one group carry out a murder every week in a different cell block. First they would start with the guys in block eight and then move right down the line, taking out every person that hung out with them. Then when that group was dead, they would carry out a prison execution on other inmates that deserved to die for whatever reason.

"How can we kill all three of these guys over in block eight at once?" Cody asked everyone. "If we kill just one, the other two will run into protective custody, and we can't let that happen."

Ramon, who lived in block eight and had watched over Sean, spoke up. "We can get all three of these fuckers at once," he said.

"How?" Cody asked.

"Let's get some bad dope with poison in it and sell it to each of them," Ramon said. "It would kill them right on the spot."

Cody liked the idea of giving them all hotshots, but suggested they make a little more of a statement. He insisted he wanted the leader, who lived on the top tier of block eight, stabbed a few extra times and thrown off onto the flats. Everyone started laughing with excitement and told Cody he was a fucking nutcase. But they loved the idea and agreed to put the plan into motion when the next drug shipment came in.

Over the next few nights in block eight, Ramon put their plan into motion by staking out the three inmates they were going to move on. They were typical prison junkies looking to get high three or four times a day. Johnny got word out to Southie that they wanted some heroin mixed with rat poison sent with some other good drugs. They received the shipment through Tony in the plate shop and adjusted the bags of bad dope so they were a little larger to tempt the junkies. Next all they had to do was get the three guys in block eight to take the bait and then watch them die.

Danny moved some of the good stuff and the five bags of bad stuff over to Ramon. Word about the new shipment got out quickly, and sure enough, one of their targets couldn't get to Ramon's cell fast enough with his money. Ramon told the guy he just got the shit in and only had one small bag on hand that he could buy for now and to come back later when the other stuff was bagged up.

The guy tossed Ramon his money and ran back to his cell to shoot up. Ramon had been smart and given him a small taste of the good shit. He knew the guys would like it so much that he would be back within a couple of hours for more.

Ramon hoped to get it to him before the cells locked down for the night. A couple of hours before count, the guy came back and Ramon sold him another, much bigger bag, hoping he would share it with his buddies. Then Ramon and his partners waited up in a room on the third tier. It was very quiet. Ramon walked down to see if the junkie was shooting up with his friends. He looked into the guy's cell and saw him lying on his bed with a needle in his arm. The guy looked dead and he hadn't shared the stuff with his friends. He had wanted the first high from the big bag before he told his pals.

Ramon returned to his partners. "We got one of them, and we have to move on at least one more before they find this guy's body."

They grabbed their gloves and walked down to one of the

other guys' cells. They asked if he wanted to try some dope, but the guy got all paranoid and said, "No I'm good."

Ramon looked at him "You got a problem buying dope from me? Or you just like killing our friend Sean?" he asked.

They jumped on the guy and grabbed his throat to stop him from yelling.

"You killed our little friend Sean, didn't you?" they said.

The guy tried to shake his head no.

"Tell me the truth and we will let you live," Ramon said.

The guy shook his head up and down, meaning yes he killed Sean. Ramon kept his arm locked around the guy's neck as his two partners stabbed the guy like a pin cushion until his body went limp. Ramon let the dead body lay on the bed. The other two continued to stab it as it lay motionless. Soon their arms grew tired from the number of times they plunged their prison shanks in and out of the guy's body. Ramon reached over with a pick and pulled out each of the dead body's eyes, tossed them in the toilet, and flushed it.

"He didn't see that coming, did he?" he told his buddies, and they laughed.

Blood was flowing steadily from the body, so they wrapped it up in the blanket and sheets and left it face-down on the bed to let it to bleed out.

They then returned to their cells to wash off the blood and take showers. After that was done, Ramon looked down to the flats and noticed the new rookie guard was just sitting there reading a book and not looking up at any of the tiers at all. Ramon and one of his partners went back to the second dead guy's room. They grabbed the body, which was wrapped up, and dragged it along the top tier. They then picked it up and tossed it off the third tier, right onto the guard's desk. As the body fell, they ran back to their cells. The guard screamed and freaked out.

All of the inmates came out of their cells, wondering what was happening. The guard fumbled for his keys, trying to get out of the block. He slammed the large gate open and closed it until more guards arrived.

All of the brass came down to the block. They looked at the body and locked down the block right away. The viciousness of the murder concerned them. Some guards tossed up their suppers when they looked more closely at the body and noticed it had no eyes. They never imagined there was another dead body in the block.

An hour later, the state police arrived to take pictures. They went cell to cell, searching for weapons and stripping the inmates to look for cuts or blood.

Suddenly a guard called out. "Open cell twenty-five. Man down."

More guards rushed up. One yelled down, "There's another dead one up here."

"Holy shit. What's happening here?" the deputy superintendent said.

It was the prison's fifth murder of the year, and they were only into the first half. Cody, Danny, and Johnny heard the banging and knew the shit had gone down. Not knowing the details, they hoped Ramon and his partners got all three of the fuckers and that nobody got busted for it.

Cody asked a guard that was taking a count what happened.

"A couple of guys just bought it over in block eight," the guard said.

Cody kicked back and smiled. *This is for you Sean*, he thought. *We will get them all, my friend. You can count on it.*

After the investigation, they kept block eight locked down and opened up the rest of the prison. They weren't sure who in block eight committed the murder, but the administration wanted to pin it on someone. The guy had been stabbed well over hundred times, and they never found his eyes. At that time they hadn't connected the two deaths. They thought the junkie overdosed on dope at the same time or that maybe the junkie committed the murder and then killed himself. They didn't know the truth and didn't have a clue.

Chapter Twenty-Four

The other three-men squads heard what happened and wanted to start moving quickly. They wanted to take out their targets the first chance they could because they wanted to confuse the prison officials and disrupt the prison's overall operations at all costs.

Danny, Cody, and Johnny had the victim in their block picked out. His name was Geno. They knew he was associated with the crew that killed Sean and were ready to move that night. They had someone sell Geno some pills earlier in the day, and he was half out of it when they entered his room that night. He was half asleep on his bed as they stood over him. Geno opened his eyes and tried to sit up but couldn't because he was off balance from the drugs. Cody hit him once and knocked him out right away. Geno fell onto his pillow.

"Let's just smother him to death," Danny said.

"That's too easy," Cody said and took a six-inch ice pick. He ran it deep into Geno's ear canal and started twisting it around and around, scrambling his brains. Johnny pulled Geno's pants down, grabbed his cock as tight as he could, and cut it off as close to the pubic hair as he could. He then pulled down Geno's chin, shoved his own cock into his mouth, and stuffed it as far down his throat he could.

"Choke on this you motherfucker," Johnny said.

They covered the dead body up to make it look like he was sleeping and left the pick in his ear and his cock down his throat. From there, they cleaned up and went to play cards on the flats of the block until supper time just to make sure the guard saw them. When it was time to go down to the mess hall, they headed out of the block and went to eat.

"Maybe they're serving hot dogs and you can watch someone choke on theirs," Cody joked to Johnny.

Johnny just laughed and shook his head.

Most of their friends sat together in the mess hall. Duke and Jimmy from the other end of the prison sat down at the table and leaned over to Cody.

"We got two more," they said.

"Two more of what?" Cody said.

Jimmy and Duke smiled. "There are two other stiffs in two different blocks down the other end of the prison and they haven't found them yet."

They didn't know Cody, Danny, and Johnny had just taken out a guy in their block. Cody looked at Danny and Johnny. "Oh shit. We are all going to hell." They all laughed.

As they walked back to the block, they heard doors start slamming. *Bam, bam, bam.* The guards yelled out to lock the prison down. They had found one of the bodies down on the other end. *They haven't found our body or the other one yet,* Cody thought.

Most of the time when the prison was locked down, the guards did a standing count. Cody's block locked down, and the guard came to Geno's room. Cody could hear him yell, "Stand up, Geno. This is a standing count." When Geno didn't stand, the guard started to threaten him. "This is my last warning to you or I'm writing you up."

No sound came from Geno, so the guard commanded the gallery to open inmate Geno's cell. After the door swung open, the guard entered the cell, pulled off the blanket, and yelled, "Son of a bitch."

The guard ran out of Geno's cell and grabbed the phone. "We have a situation here in block seven."

You got more than a situation, buddy, Cody thought to himself.

Then, disguising his voice, fucking Johnny yelled down, "Looks like you can't write him up for not standing, fucknuts." The block started cracking up.

State police and prison officials learned three more murders had taken place all in one day and couldn't figure out what was going on. They locked the prison down for months and cleaned house. They put over two hundred inmates either in the segregation unit or transferred them to other institutions under tight security and held them there until they got some information on what was going on. They thought it might be gang wars within the institution.

The prison was in a lockdown like never before. The authorities were concerned not just about inmates getting murdered, but also how brutally they were being tortured. The authorities knew whoever committed the crimes had gotten enjoyment out of their work. They never suspected the culprits were execution squads working as groups, but they knew something big was happening and that they had to put a stop to it all.

The state police interviewed people every day. When they pulled Cody down to the interview room, the state trooper kept staring him. Finally he said, "You don't remember me do you, Cody?"

Cody looked at him. "You look familiar," he said.

"I'm Trooper Mark Chase from your old neighborhood. Remember on the Mass Turnpike when I took that starters pistol off you and you had all those keys?"

"Hell yes, I remember you," Cody said. "So what brings you here to the prison today, Mark?"

Trooper Chase smiled. "I see that over all this time you never lost your sense of humor, have you?" He explained to Cody that he worked for the district attorney's office in that county and now handled all investigation for the prisons.

Cody smiled at him. "So, Mark, what are investigating today?"

"Stop it, Cody. I'm not amused," Trooper Chase said. "You

must of heard or know something about these murders. I'm sure you know about Geno dying in your block, and if you know anything, I can get you a great deal, Cody. I can get you transferred out of here back to a minimum prison and put a word in for the parole board down the road. Just help me out here, Cody. Tell me anything, and I'll help you out.

Cody looked at him straight in the eye. "Chase, did you forget were we both come from?" He smiled. Then he told Trooper Chase that he knew nothing at that time, but if he heard anything maybe they could talk again.

Trooper Chase told Cody to just ask to see him and he would come right up. Cody agreed and went back to his cell.

The prison stayed in lockdown for a total of six months and slowly reopened one block each week. The officials hoped the removal of inmates to the segregation unit and other prisons would bring the murders to a halt and that the investigations would bring murder indictments to those responsible.

Cody and his group stayed locked up in segregation on charges that they were disrupting the running of the institution. It was a bullshit charge, but the prison officials could charge them with whatever they wanted to in prison. Cody and his friends knew they couldn't be locked up in the segregation unit forever on charges like that.

They sat back and made the best of things while they were locked up twenty-three hours a day, and nobody talked about the murders. They were worried the place was wired or someone might overhear them talking.

Chapter Twenty-Five

Eight months passed. On a cold Monday morning, Cody heard a lot of movement in the hallway. Guards were going to certain cells with chains and leg irons. They took Cody, Danny, and Johnny out first and chained them. The guards escorted them outside, where they had several prison police cars lined up. They loaded the three of them into one car. Cody then saw all of the other inmates, shackled in groups of three, being escorted out and placed into cars. No one knew what the hell was going on.

"Where the hell are we going?" Cody shouted.

The guards didn't say a word and as the cars pulled out of the prison gates. They could see all of the state troopers escorting the prison cars to an unknown destination. Their sirens blared all the way down the highway.

Cody, Danny, and Johnny remained silent for the whole ride. Soon, they looked ahead and realized where they were going. The courthouse looked like an armed fortress with all the cops that surrounded it. Cody and his partners were the first to get out of the line of cars, and the news people tried to get photos of them as they were escorted into the courthouse.

They went straight into the courtroom, where the judge read from a paper stating a grand jury had found cause against the three of them for murdering and mutilating Geno Baber. He asked them if any of them had an attorney. They said they didn't. The judge gave them lists to pick attorneys from and the court set a date for them to enter their plea.

Out they went, and in came another three prisoners for more murder indictments. The district attorney's office went crazy that day. He indicted twenty-one people all in one day. It made headline news all over the country. He was quoted in newspapers as saying he had twenty-one inmates indicted for running execution squads within a prison. The inmates were shocked at how the prick had been able to come up with any good informants because he didn't even have the right people for the right murders. Some of the guys he indicted didn't know anything about what had happened and had never associated with Cody or his group.

Now, Cody thought to himself, *we have to find out who the informant was that is testifying against us.* Danny and Johnny knew that nobody had seen anything that day. By time they got back to the prison, they also knew none of them had a chance of getting out of the segregation unit any time soon. As soon as they got back to their cells, the prison officials charged them with disciplinary charges for murder just so it would get added to their prison records.

Cody picked a great lawyer from the list the court gave him. He knew a little about the guy and that he was one of the best in the state and was very street smart. Cody and the guys knew they wouldn't get to trial for at least nine months to a year, and they knew everyone would know the names of the D.A.'s prison informants within a few months when their lawyers filed paperwork through the court.

Sure enough, three months later the attorneys found out who was testifying against each group. The prison officials had come up with a guy from Cody's block who swore he remembered seeing Cody, Danny, and Johnny walking out of Geno's room. He even lied, stating he saw Danny with blood all over his body.

They knew it was bullshit, and that it was going to be a long stay in the segregation unit. Ramon and Duke took over Cody's connections and even had Tony from the plate shop keep bringing in drugs. Ramon kept a supply of drugs coming up to the segregation unit and pot for Cody to smoke just to help make the time pass.

Cody, Danny, and Johnny couldn't understand why the other eighteen guys had been indicted along with them. They had no association with Cody and his group. But Ramon, Duke, and some of the boys out in population were happy about how everything worked because none of them had been indicted or lugged to the segregation unit. They knew the other innocent inmates might go down for what they did. Everyone knew the informants the district attorney had were just playing him and making everything up to get a out of jail free cards for testifying and lying like rugs.

The days couldn't come quick enough for Cody, Danny, and Johnny to go to trial. Their trial would be up first before the other murder cases the district attorney had on his plate. Finally, a jury was chosen and they were ready to start trial. Cody and his partners' attorneys ripped the case apart. And as far as the informant went, Cody's attorney asked him where he had been standing when he saw Cody, Danny, and Johnny come out of Geno's room. The dumb bastard said he was down on the flats and just happened to look up and saw them walk out of Geno's room all bloody.

Little did the informant know that the attorneys had taken the jury inside the prison to the blocks where the crimes occurred. The jury had seen the flats where he claimed to have been standing. Then Cody's attorney asked the informant if he cut a deal to get out of prison in exchange for his testimony. He looked down at the floor and said yes, they will set him free for his testimony.

"No more questions," the attorney said, and that was all it took.

The jury knew for a fact someone couldn't see up to that cell from where the informant said he'd been standing. They knew he was lying. The trial lasted for a total of ten days, and the district attorney's star witness looked like shit on the stand. That was the district attorney's whole case, that one informant. They had no other facts at all.

The jury stepped out and returned an hour later with their verdict. They found Cody, Danny, and Johnny not guilty. Word traveled back to the prison faster than Cody and his partners. The inmates were happier than pigs in shit. The district attorney's office was pissed and knew they had to regroup. They knew they could not bring the other inmates to trial and spend tax payers' money and lose more trials. The district attorney dropped all of the grand jury indictments against the other inmates after Cody and his partners beat theirs because they were all weak cases.

Chapter Twenty-Six

The district attorney's office had never had a conviction for any murders in that particular maximum security prison, going all the way back to the 1960s. Getting grand jury indictment was easy, but getting a conviction by a jury was the hard part. They needed a witness that was believable and convincing, one that knew all the facts.

The prison officials were dumbfounded by what happened, and knew they had to let everybody back out into the prison population again. All of the drummed charges meant nothing, and all it did was keep everyone locked up and out of population. They slowly released each and every inmate that beat the murder charges, case by case, back into population and placed them all in one prison block.

As happy as Cody, Danny, and Johnny were that they beat the charges, it had been a long stretch in the segregation unit for them all. Even the innocent guys had been held up in there for the whole time, and the year and a half of being locked up twenty-three hours a day messed up everyone's heads. Danny had started to use a lot more drugs, and they all came out more paranoid than when they went in.

All that Cody and his partners had built up in the prison was lost. Ramon and Duke were running everything now. Cody had no more control over drugs, extortion, or any of the booking. The officials watched Cody and his partners closely. If they messed up, they knew they would be taken back to the segregation unit for any small reason. All they had going for them was their reputation as killers in one of the worst prisons in the country.

The good news was that Johnny was up for parole. Who would have believed it? They gave him a parole with a stipulation that he had to do three months in a halfway house with counseling. The reasoning behind the stipulation was that it would help Johnny adjust his mind for the street life. Cody couldn't be happier. He gave his friend a big hug and told him it was his big shot to be free once again.

Tear came to Johnny's eyes. He didn't want to leave Cody behind. He made a bunch of plans for Cody, telling him he would break him out and how they would all be together again like the old days. Cody smiled and told him to stay in touch, get his act together, and try to get away from shooting drugs. It would be good to have Johnny out on the street. He would be a very dependable connection for Cody, but Cody feared Johnny was not going to make it out there. He had nothing and nobody out there for him. Cody knew he was being set up to fail the moment he hit the streets.

Cody was now twenty eight years old and had close to eleven years in the system and realized he had less than four more years himself until he saw the parole board. He knew he had better get his shit together and find a way to get down to a lower prison status before he saw the board. There was no way the board would consider his release if he was still in a maximum security prison. Cody thought about how he could get transferred somewhere else in the prison system. Even though the jury found him not guilty of the murder charge, he would always be guilty in the eyes of the Department of Correction.

Danny had another year before he saw the board, but he was shooting drugs three to five times a day and had totally lost it from being locked up in the segregation unit. He couldn't care less about seeing the board or anything else. He just wanted to get high and get his mind free from the prison bullshit.

Months flew by, and guys came and went. Nobody knew who was who anymore. Cody kept putting in for transfers and kept getting shot down. The prison had a new class of inmates there now. Cody still had people he hung with, but everything had changed. Ramon and Duke were still running everything, but they still had Cody's back.

Two months later, Cody got news that Johnny had been shot and died out on the streets. He read the paper the next day and read a story about Johnny getting into an argument with a guy at a bar. Johnny grabbed a knife and tried to stab the guy, and the guy pulled out gun and shot him dead. Cody couldn't believe it. He had grown up with Johnny, and they shared everything. Now his favorite person in the world was dead.

Cody understood people out on the streets didn't take prison bullshit out there. Johnny's head had been too messed up from his long stay in the segregation unit to just walk out of a maximum security prison and right onto the streets. It would mess up anyone's thoughts. Cody thought of how Johnny had made it through all of the prison shit, walked out, made it to a halfway house, just to get killed on the streets in the short time he was free.

Cody had a hard time comprehending any of it and felt bad for Johnny. *But at least he died on the streets and not in this hellhole*, Cody thought. When he told Danny about it, Danny was all drugged up and said to Cody, "Fuck him. We all got to die sometime," and then reached for more drugs. He stuck the needle in his arm. "We will all be with him soon," he said as he nodded off.

Cody leaned toward Danny. "No fucking way," he told him. "I refuse to die in this fucking prison." He grabbed a couple of bags of dope from Danny's stash, cooked both bags together, dropped in a cotton ball, and absorbed it through the needle. He grabbed Danny's arm, found one of his veins, and shot him up with the shit, leaving the needle in his arm. "Go join my friends and brothers, Johnny and Sean, now." He left the room with tears in his eyes.

Later that day, they found Danny dead from an overdose with the needle Cody had left still in his arm. As Cody looked back at all the violence and all the inmate deaths, he asked himself if it was all worth doing. He still looked back and thought about his little friend Sean, and he believed he did Danny a favor. Cody now was totally lost and withdrew from everyone in the prison. When he walked the yard, he walked alone, looking for answers. Other inmates left him alone, believing he was just sad over the deaths of Johnny and Danny.

They knew Cody had a right to be sad. They knew his past and what he had built within the prison walls. He had fought the system as best as he could and had never given up on wanting to be free. But they all knew he was growing weaker and that it would only be a matter of time before the day would come when he died within the prison walls.

Chapter Twenty-Seven

Over the years, inmates lost it, and the prison officials tightened up the security more and more. Ramon, Duke, and the group was getting tired of the prison administration and the new superintendent busting their balls, watching their every move, and not letting them move around like they use to. Everyone in the group had reached the end of their ropes. Ramon, Duke, and a few others wanted to make a statement by killing the prison's new superintendent. They also wanted to get back at some of the guards for all the bullshit they'd had to put up with. They wanted to do it not by just taking them hostage, but by fucking stabbing or killing them.

"So what you are saying is, we are all going to commit suicide because the swat teams will come in and kill us all," Cody said to everyone.

"We are already fucking dead," Ramon yelled. "You think you're ever getting out of this prison alive, Cody? And I want you to remember, Cody, nobody ever complained when you wanted to start whacking out other inmates in the prison over Sean's death."

"That was different," Cody snapped.

"How is it any different?" Ramon demanded, challenging Cody.

Cody stood there. He didn't have an answer. He knew Ramon was right.

"See," yelled Ramon. "You don't have a fucking answer for me, do you Cody? We're going to do this with or without you. We can't keep living like this. If the guards want a fucking war, let's give them one. Let get as many of these fuckers as we can, and

I'm going to cut that fucking superintendent's head off myself. It will teach every prison administration in the country that they can only fuck with inmates for so long."

Ramon had everyone crying for blood. Their main target was the prison superintendent. He would be easy to get because he stood out in front of the mess hall with his deputies every day at lunchtime.

Cody didn't say anything and just listened. He knew it was not open for a discussion. It was going to happen with or without him. Everyone started planning, and they all agreed to bring a massive amount of drugs into the prison and get the whole population wasted, which wouldn't be hard to do at all. Starting a riot would be easy. The whole prison would be down for that, but nobody except forty to sixty of them would know what was really going to happen: their group of inmates would grab, stab, and kill anyone wearing a prison uniform.

Ramon looked at Cody. "You're down with this, right Cody?" he asked.

Cody smiled. He understood how angry everybody was, and he'd had enough. "Fucking right, I'm down with you guys, just like you all were there for me," he shouted.

Cody couldn't believe the excitement and happiness in everyone's eyes at his support of Ramon. It looked like all of the stress was released from their bodies. They wanted revenge for being locked up in the segregation unit and for all the shit they'd had to put up with from the system. Cody did understand, but he knew they would all lose.

Ramon hugged him and thanked him for his support. He then told Cody he was going to give Tony five grand to bring in a gun. Ramon had told Tony that if he didn't, he would have his family killed.

"Is he going to do it?" Cody asked.

"He already brought me in the bullets," Ramon said and gave Cody one for good luck. He told him how Tony got them in by the gatehouse. Only Ramon, Duke, and Cody would know about the gun.

The plan was in effect. They ordered the drugs from the streets. Ramon had well over ten thousand downers coming in, and the inmates were making weapons in the prison metal shop, including an ax to bury in the superintendent's fucking head. They planned to pick a day at lunchtime to walk out of the mess hall and start stabbing the officials right away, while other inmates stabbed as many guards as they could in each block and in the hallways.

They also agreed that after that was done, they would kill some of the inmates they thought were rats, rapists, and pedophiles. They had to make sure all the drugs, mostly downers, were passed throughout the prison a day or two before it was to take place. All of the drugs would be free, that way most of the population would act off the drugs' effects.

Two weeks passed, and Cody was getting very concerned. He knew it was really going to happen, and he knew what the outcome would be—certain death to most of the inmates, including himself. The guards and swat teams wouldn't get inside quick enough to save any of the staff. The superintendent and guards would be dead within ten minutes. The prisoners would set massive fires in all the shops and that would be it.

The officials outside the prison would just think it was just a riot with hostages taken. By the time they had their shit set up and were ready to come inside the prison, it would be hours later. They would want to start negotiations first, and when the state police and prison swat teams would enter the prison and find out the staff had been mass murdered, there would be no negotiating at all. It would be open season on most of the inmates inside.

Ramon and Duke met with Cody and told him how everything was to go down in two weeks. It would happen on a Friday at noon, and they already had ten thousand pills coming in that very day. Cody asked Ramon what the plan was when police and swat teams entered the prison.

"Who gives a shit," Ramon said. "We will all be too wasted to give two shits about anything."

Cody asked Ramon about the gun. "Did you get it in?"

Ramon just smiled "If you hear a big bang in the fucking hallway, that will answer your question," he told Cody.

Cody smiled back and told Ramon he would help put out the word for people to get ready, but he just went back to his cell and never said anything to anyone. Cody wanted nothing to do with the plan and knew he couldn't stop it. It was too big for even him to control. He didn't have any more say in the prison. For the first time in his life, he started to worry.

He knew that some of the guys planning that shit didn't want to live anymore and were going to overdose themselves and take as many people as they could with them. The others were just fed up with the system. Starting trouble in prison and getting everyone worked up was always easy, but most of the population didn't understand what was really going to happen. They were all going to be used. Cody had reached his wits end and didn't want anything to do with any of the bullshit. He understood more than those crazy bastards did.

He couldn't sleep. He burned out his brain thinking as the days sped by. He kept looking at the fucking bullet in his hand. His head was fucked up after being locked up for so long in the segregation unit, but he still understood more than those crazy bastards.

Cody watched as the drugs were slowly passed throughout the prison. Finally, it hit him. He couldn't do it. He couldn't go through with Ramon's stupid plan. First, he thought maybe he could try to take out Ramon, but thought better of it because he always had too many guys around him. Plus, Ramon lived over in another block. Cody knew it would be too hard.

Then he started thinking about how he could make it work for himself. He wondered what would happen if he contacted his old pal, Trooper Chase. Something good could come of it. He could make a deal and get his ass of that shithole prison. But then he thought there was no way they would ever let him out of prison and back to the streets with just this information.

Chapter Twenty-Eight

Cody knew his information was worth its weight in gold, but he had never ratted on anyone before and knew his life would be in danger if he did. He wasn't sure how to go about it. If he worked with the state police and told them what was going down, he knew it would be stopped. Cody also knew that if he talked to them, they would want to know everything he knew about all of the murders. That was the only way he would have a shot at regaining his freedom. Cody felt backed into a corner, but he knew he had to go for it.

He couldn't trust any of the guards or the prison administration. They couldn't give Cody the kind of a deal he was looking for, and some of the guards might go back and tell Ramon's people. If that happened, Cody would be killed on the spot. So, he came up with a plan to contact Trooper Chase. He would come out of the mess hall at lunchtime, walk by the deputy superintendent, tell him he had to speak to Trooper Chase right away, and then keep walking. Cody knew it had to be today.

That afternoon, he went to lunch and sat with Ramon and Duke.

"Everything alright?" Ramon asked Cody.

Cody told them he was a little down and needed to get high after lunch. "I'll feel better after that," he said.

"Well," Ramon said, "come out in the yard and we will all get high together."

Cody smiled and agreed to meet them. He waited until they left the mess hall first and then made his move. He started to walk out of the mess hall and made eye contact with the deputy.

He walked up to him, made a turn and spoke as fast he as could, "Get Trooper Chase up here today for me. I want to speak with him now." He turned back and walked away.

The deputy superintendent could not believe what he'd just heard from Cody. And as Cody walked away, he glanced back and saw the deputy walking quickly into the control room. Cody went back to his cell and didn't bother going out to meet Ramon and Duke.

He waited and waited all that day and heard nothing. He started to get nervous and didn't know what was happening. He even missed supper. He didn't want to run into Ramon and Duke and have to answer any more of their questions. And then that night about 6:30 PM, the guard called up to Cody from the flats, "Hey Cody, you have a visit."

Cody's heart started pumping. A visit? Who could be visiting him? He showered, got dressed, and headed to the visiting room. As Cody walked through one main door to visiting room, two guards stopped him and handcuffed him.

"What is happening here?" Cody asked.

They ordered him not to say anything and not to make a scene. The guards brought Cody out to the front main lobby and to the superintendent's office. They walked Cody inside and there stood Trooper Mark Chase with the superintendent and his deputy. They removed the handcuffs, and Cody sat down.

"Cody, I got word you want to speak to me right away, and I know something has to be really wrong if you want to talk to me," Trooper Chase said.

Cody was quiet for a moment and then requested to speak to him alone. The two prison officials stepped out of the room.

"Look Chase, something is going down. It's big, and I want nothing to do with it, but I want something in return for this information."

"What do you want, Cody?" Trooper Chase asked.

"My freedom, and I'll take nothing less," Cody stated. "And

I want the additional sentencing time I received from the escapes also removed."

Trooper Chase sat back for a moment. He fumbled with a pencil on the desk and then looked at Cody. "That is a real tall order you're asking for, Cody. I know you know everything about all the murders in here. Are you ready to tell my boss everything you know and take everything to trial and get him some convictions?"

"Yes," Cody answered.

"Once you cross over, Cody, there is no turning back," Chase told him.

Again, Cody agreed.

"I already spoke to my boss the district attorney's office about tonight's meeting," Chase said. "He wanted me to give you a message that if you were looking for any kind of a deal, he would give you what you wanted with full immunity from anything you were involved in, but you have to assure him you will deliver some murder convictions from this joint and take a polygraph test."

Trooper Chase also told Cody it would have to be everything he had. He wanted to know about every murder, down to the smallest detail. Cody told him it was hard for him because he had never ratted on anyone in his life, but he agreed and said he wanted everything in writing. He also requested they supply him with his own attorney for the agreement.

Trooper Chase grabbed the phone and spoke to the district attorney.

"It's a go," he told his boss. "He is requesting it in writing, and we need to get him a lawyer tonight. We will meet you at the state police barracks in one hour."

Trooper Chase stood up and brought the superintendent into the room. "We will need to take him to the state police barracks now. I don't believe he will be coming back here."

"He'll need two correction officers for escorts," the superintendent stated.

"No guards!" Cody exclaimed. "You'll blow everything. They don't know how to keep their mouths shut."

"You can trust my guards I have here," the superintendent told Cody.

"You think so," Cody said. "Wait till you hear what I have to tell you."

The deputy superintendent stepped in and said he would be the escort. He understood something big was going on and he wanted to be part of it.

"Okay, I'll go with you," the superintendent said and ordered a car brought to the front of the prison.

Chase called in a couple of state troopers in for an escort. They took Cody and placed him in the back seat of the prison car and took him to the state police barracks where a special unit of state police was waiting for him to arrive.

Chapter Twenty-Nine

Once in the barracks, they sat Cody down, and then the district attorney showed up with his people and a lawyer for Cody. They went over the agreement. Cody had to give them all the facts about the prison murders and everything else he knew. Then, after they were convinced what he was saying was true, he would testify. They would speak at his parole board meeting and talk to the governor's office about his parole, and he would be fully exonerated of all charges for his testimony and would be paid as a state police informant.

Cody sat reading the document he had to sign word by word. *So this is how the other side works,* he thought to himself. *This is how they get inmates to lie and make up stories just to get a few convictions for their glory.* Trooper Chase placed his hand on Cody's shoulder.

"What was wrong?" Chase asked.

Cody smiled and said he was new to this and was just making sure everything was covered. "What about my safety? Where am I going until this is over?" Cody asked.

They told him Trooper Chase and the commissioner of correction would work together and bounce him around from jail to jail every month until it was all over.

"What's wrong?" Trooper Chase asked Cody again. He looked Cody in the eye. "I will give you my word, I'll ride this out with you ever step of the way. Trust me, my old friend. You know me from the old days. I haven't changed. If I burn you, my word will never be worth anything."

Cody smiled and signed the paperwork, and everything was

agreed upon. They turned on their recorders, and Trooper Chase stated, "Let's get started. What was the reason you asked to speak to me today, Cody? What is going on in the prison?"

Cody started to tell them about the takeover and what was going to happen the following Friday. He explained step by step how the takeover of the prison was going to happen. Then he gave up names and where most of the weapons could be found. He told them about all the drugs in the prison and where there group stashed everything and that there was also talk about a couple of guns being brought in.

He walked them through the plan step by step. The prison superintendent jumped on the phone and spoke to the commissioner of correction and then called down to the prison and had them call in everyone that worked there and lockdown the whole fucking joint.

"How can any one inmate bring ten thousand pills into my prison in one day?" the superintendent asked Cody very sarcastically. He laughed at the idea that any inmate could ever get a gun inside of his prison. "I find that one hard to believe," the superintendent said out loud, and others started to smile along with him. "I think you're wasting everyone's time here and looking for a free ride on something you can't deliver."

Cody looked at Trooper Chase, stood up shaking his head, and smiled right back at the superintendent. "Well, I'll tell you what, Mr. Superintendent, since you and everyone here thinks this is so funny, if you go to my room I have one of the bullets, a .22 hidden in the edge of my mattress, and Ramon and Duke have two hundred more."

Nobody in the room was smiling now. No one said a word. The superintendent jumped on the phone again and ordered the guards at the prison to pull Cody's mattress out of his room and rip apart. He received a call back not long after. They found the bullet.

"Holy shit," he said in disbelief. "Who brought the gun in and how?"

Cody noticed they were starting to panic. A fucking gun in

a prison was big. Cody told them about Tony in the plate shop and how he always brought a metal lunch box to work with him. He had placed the bullets in a baggie wrapped in duck tape in his thermos. Then Cody gave them Tony's address and told them that was where they dropped off all the prison's drugs. He told them Tony had been collecting over a grand a week from their group and that he had made tens of thousands of dollars in cash over the years. He also told them about a medic in the prison some other guys were using to get shit in from the streets.

Next, he informed them about the guards that transported drugs up to the segregation unit and throughout the prison. Cody even told them about selling the dealers plates from the prison. The deputy was really pissed off at Tony because they lived in the same town and sometimes commuted into work together.

Their attention was locked on to every word Cody had to say about the prison takeover, and they understood why he had come forward. They knew he felt like he was backed into corner, and there had to be other inmates inside the prison that felt the same way. The superintendent told Trooper Chase the commissioner was calling the governor and would be requesting two hundred state police in full gear outside the prison in four hours. The National Guard would be on standby if they needed federal transfers.

"Let's have Tony picked up right now and see how many guns that prick brought into the prison and find out what else has been going on," Trooper Chase said. "And let's pick up that prison medic, too. Bring them both here to this barracks. If they try to deny anything, we will have them see Cody. And then they will know how we have the information."

Before even getting into the other details of what Cody knew, they agreed to stop for the night and concentrate on the issue of the takeover and take all necessary action before anyone got hurt. They told Cody he would be sleeping the next couple of nights at the barracks and that Trooper Chase would retrieve him over the next couple of days to continue their meeting down the district attorney's office.

Chapter Thirty

Trooper Chase showed up the later the next day and told Cody about all the shit they found at the prison. They would be going through the prison with a fine-tooth comb over the next few months. They had ripped the place apart. Everyone was taken to the segregation unit and interviewed. Other inmates even came forward about the takeover and the riot, but not too many had known about the killings.

They found the ax and as many as two thousand weapons and the mother lode of pills. They even found a list of names in Ramon's cell that said what officers they wanted to kill first, and who to torture, and whose heads to remove. They found over two hundred bullets, and Tony confessed to everything. He hadn't gotten the gun inside yet. He was going to try to get it in that week and claimed he'd done it because his family was in danger.

Trooper Chase told Cody he had done a great job and saved many lives.

"You know, not to many guys made it out of the old neighborhood," he said to Cody with a smile. "Most have either moved out, are dead, or are still in prison." He told Cody about how many times the older gangsters tried to bribe him to go over to their side back when he and Cody first met. The temptation had always been there, but he told them to go fuck themselves every time. He never sold out and liked being a cop.

"What you think of me selling out?" Cody asked him.

Again he smiled. "You have your whole life ahead of you. You'll do well." He promised Cody he would keep his word and that they would become the best of friends and he would always be there for him. "But if you fuck me over, all bets are off."

"Does anybody know I am the informant yet?" Cody asked.

"No way," Chase said. "Everybody is being bounced around, and the prison will be shut down for a while." He then went on to say, "They are thinking about getting some of these psychos off to the federal prisons all over the country. They will not find out about you for months. As far as they're concerned, you were taken to a federal prison somewhere in east bum fuck."

Cody understood everything perfectly. They went to the district attorney's office and sat in an office that could hold about fifteen people. The district attorney thanked Cody for the information on the prison and for saving people's lives. He walked over and shook Cody's hand. "Which direction are we going in today?"

"Let's start off with the places where all the drugs came from the street and into the prison," Cody said. That day, he gave up four key labs out in the street and gave up a several more crooked guards inside the prison.

Trooper Chase got warrants and the state police together with other agencies and raided the labs the next day. They also made more arrests back at the prison. The newspapers wrote about the district attorney like he was on a one-man crusade. He was looking very good in the public's eye. With the prison takeover, the hope they were going to turn it around once and for all, and the arrest of the labs and the crooked staff at the prison, they all knew he would be a walk-in for the upcoming district elections.

Not only did the D.A. want to get back into the office, but that prick was looking down the road at Washington, D.C., and getting into the House or Senate. He was a typical politician. Cody knew if he moved up, all the people who helped get him there would get a piece of the pie, but Cody just wanted to be free. He vowed never to go back to prison. He was a man now, and at age thirty, he'd had enough. All of his close friends were dead, and he had nobody to fall back on. He was alone and need to find another outlet in life. He was fighting to live again.

Chapter Thirty-One

The district attorney wanted to know about the real shit that happened with the murders. He knew it would take weeks or months to get all the information together before they could bring it to the grand jury. They started out by first asking Cody what he knew about Frankie and his crew member Louie. They wanted to know who killed each of them. Out of all of the murders that had happened in the prison, they needed to know about those two first.

Cody lied and told them he knew nothing about Frankie's murder. Even though Cody had full immunity, he had to lie. Cody didn't want his name out there for being involved in killing a mob guy. He knew the mob would never forget Frankie's murder and would order a hit on Cody if he ever confessed to killing him. He knew it would only be a matter of time before someone put a bullet in his head, and the state police could not protect him forever.

Cody told them he heard it was someone from his crew, and it was a decision from the streets. But with Louie, he told them Danny and Johnny committed the murder because they wanted his drugs. Cody said he only found out about it after they reopened the blocks up. He told them Danny was a very big junkie and needed his fix five times a day. He added that Danny had felt so bad over Johnny's death that he overdosed.

Cody didn't care. Johnny and Danny were both dead, and he didn't want to implicate himself as being present while everyone was killed. He knew if he told them he had planned and carried out most of the murders they wouldn't keep their deal. They'd find another way to fuck him over and not let him back on the street. He also knew what he had to do. Just play them slowly, put a lot of the blame on other inmates, and sound very convincing.

The district attorney slapped his hands hard on the table and got right in Cody's face. "Are you going to sit here and just feed me shit? I can't convict dead people. I want the murdering bastards, the cold blooded motherfuckers who butchered these other guys and the leaders. I want to bring them into the courthouse and get all guilty verdicts and nothing less. I know you were in the middle of all this shit, so you better take a moment and think what might come out of your mouth on your next statement to me, Cody."

Cody very calmly sat back in his chair. "Look, instead of asking me this and that, let me tell you who did what and how it all went down, and then you can ask all the questions you want."

The D.A. regained his composure and apologized. "Yes, let's do it your way, Cody. Let's take a lunch break start over again in an hour."

Trooper Chase walked over to Cody and told him. "Stop trying to play these people. They're not stupid, and they'll bury you. I would hate to see that happen at this stage of the game."

Everyone regrouped after lunch, and Cody said, "Let's start with the two murders down the other end of the prison. Ramon was the leader of all the groups. He made most of the decisions on who died and what day. He had Duke, Eddie, and Jimmy take out Manny Davila. They had Pat, Ronnie, and Billy take out Chris Biz. And me, Danny, and Johnny carried out that execution of the guy in my block, Geno Baber, of which we were found not guilty."

Cody explained how Ramon not only planned the uprising of the prison, but how he also demanded murders to be carried out to keep order and keep fear in the other inmates and ensure that only his group ran everything. He made it clear to everyone that Ramon called the shots over the past two years and that Cody was only one key member in the group and he had followed orders, just like everyone else. He made it very clear that nobody fucked with their group.

He also explained how they ran all the extortion, blackmail, booking, and drugs, and not just in the maximum prison, but in the medium prisons as well. Cody confessed to beating the guy with the weight down in the other prison, but he claimed it had been in self-defense after the beating he took. He explained that if someone wanted a guy beaten, piped, or stabbed from the streets or from another prison, all they had to do was contact anyone in the group and it would be done for either money or a favor in return.

Cody remembered one incident when a friend of theirs named Teddy was up in the segregation unit and another inmate named Henry had given him a lot of shit while he was in there with him. Teddy sent out word that he wanted Henry taught a lesson and just wanted him piped or beaten. They sent word back to him asking what if the guy got killed by accident. He sent back word to them saying, "Well, if you kill him, you kill him."

So as Henry walked by them in the prison yard, Jackie ran up behind him and hit him in the head with a fifteen-inch pipe and cracked the guy's skull open. It had sounded like a bat hitting a baseball. They could hear the sound a hundred yards away in the prison yard.

The assistant district attorney, Donna Stevens, who would be running all the trials, asked Cody if he felt any remorse about what happened within the prison walls. Cody looked into her eyes and said, "Are you kidding me? Remorse about what? This is the way it is in prison. It's a hellhole. People die, people get hurt, and people do drugs just to escape into another world. There is no love or feeling for anyone. People get on each other's nerves, and even though the prison has rules, the only rule each and every inmate has is to watch their own back and get the hell out any way they can."

"Is this why you felt you had to escape and be such a burden on the prison system and society?" she asked Cody.

"That's very simple," Cody said to her with a cocky attitude. He told her he never wanted to become institutionalized and didn't want to do his time. He felt better being free with some nice hot chick and doing whatever he felt like. He told her he never understood why all the other inmates just stayed there and did their time.

Then she got more aggressive and told Cody, "You had nothing out in the streets. What was the real reason you escaped?"

"Just to do it," he replied.

"That's not good enough for me," she shouted and again tried to push his buttons, looking for his weak spot. Trooper Chase was watching from the corner. He knew her method of getting Cody to snap.

"As far as me being a burden on the prison system and society, that's how I survived in prison and made a name for myself," Cody told her and then asked, "Why are you being such a bitch toward me? When is the last time you got laid?"

She didn't even blink an eye at Cody's question. She turned so she stood face to face with him. "You are no better than the inmates we are going to try and get convicted on these charges," she shouted. "You have no feeling toward anyone, and I don't think you even like yourself or anyone else. Isn't that right, Cody? You never liked anyone in your life, did you? You're the one with issues, and in my opinion, I believe we shouldn't even help you be released from prison."

And that was it. She had found Cody's weak spot.

"Don't sit here and judge me," he shouted. "You have no fucking idea what it was like being locked up in prison day in and day out, not even counting the years I spent in segregation.

Everybody I ever liked or got close to in my life either got murdered or died."

He told them all about his friend Sean, and how the young kid had come into a fucked up prison system and was killed for no reason by two assholes in block eight that just wanted to prey on a weak kid. He told them how the system and the prison officials didn't protect his young friend by transferring him out of that maximum prison.

"Is that why that inmate was stabbed over one hundred and forty times and tossed off the third story tier?" she asked.

Cody stood up in tears. "Fucking right. That young kid got killed and nobody cared. You people here at the district attorney's office and state police didn't do a fucking thing about it and just wrote it off like just another murder. Let me tell you something, he was a good kid and he was my friend and he was someone I let close to me. And I saw to it that prison justice was carried out to those responsible for killing Sean."

"Did you order the murders?" she then asked,

"I didn't do anything to stop it!" Cody shouted.

"That was not my question to you," she snapped back, looking right into Cody's eyes. "Did you order the murders, Cody?"

Tears rolled down Cody's face as he yelled, "Yes, I was a part of making the decision. I wanted those fuckers dead more than anyone. Ramon came up with the plan to take out three inmates in the block that day. And, as matter of fact, Ramon carried out the two executions in block eight. There should have been three that day.

"We all agreed to set the junkies up and sell the bad dope to the three fuckers that killed Sean. Tony brought in the bad dope and assumed it was just his regular delivery and when Ramon couldn't get the other two guys to shoot the bad dope, he settled for stabbing and tossing the guy off the tier.

"Yes, we all knew when and how it was going to happen, and let me tell you something, lady, I'm fucking glad those two motherfuckers died that day. The only thing I'm sorry about is that I couldn't do it myself. I wanted to see their faces and let them both know Sean was my friend and someone I cared about. They killed him for fucking nothing. They had no reason at all to kill my little friend."

The room was silent. The assistant district attorney looked at Cody and asked her final two questions in a normal tone of voice. "What happened to the inmate's eyes?"

"Ramon flushed them down the toilet," he answered.

"I see you have tears in your eyes, Cody. I think you're showing a little remorse about what happened."

"Yes, a little," Cody said. "The tears are for my little buddy Sean because even after getting Sean's murderers, I realize it still will never bring him back."

"One last question for my own knowledge, Cody, when you guys went in and killed Geno, why did you castrate him? What was the statement you were trying to make by placing his gentiles down his throat?"

"All the murders were all about making a statement," Cody told her. "We wanted to get a point across to everyone in their group about Sean's death, and we wanted to put fear in the whole prison system. Nobody touches anyone in our group ever."

She thanked Cody. "Believe it or not," she told him. "What you're doing now will assure other inmates like your friend Sean. They will have a chance of leaving prison alive. You're going to turn the whole prison system around for the better when everything is done."

Then she told Cody, "Did you know your group had people scared of entering that prison just to serve their time? We were getting letters from inmates pleading us to help get them transferred."

"I never want another younger inmate to go through what Sean did," Cody said. "So, I do hope something good happens out of this."

Trooper Chase stepped in. "Why don't we all take a break and start again tomorrow? I'll bring Cody up to the barracks and let him get cleaned up, and he'll be nice and refreshed in the morning."

Chase walked to the car with Cody and asked him, "Are you alright?"

Cody nodded yes.

"You need to relax. They are pushing your buttons just to see how much pressure you can take and were your weak points are. When they put you on the stand, remember one thing Cody, one lie leads to another."

Then Chase explained to Cody that was why they never got murder convictions from the prisons. All of their informants got messed up on the stand because of a lie, and they couldn't handle the pressure. "But you, Cody, you know word for word what happened and how it happened. You were there. Just tell the truth and be yourself. You will be fine."

Cody didn't say a word in the car during the whole ride back to the barracks. Trooper Chase knew how Cody felt about getting those two guys in block eight that killed his young friend Sean. It was like street justice. It was going to be done, and nobody was going to stop it.

Chapter Thirty-Two

The state police administered a lie detector test to Cody after what he told everyone. They asked all basic questions about the murders. Chase wrote the questions for the test, and they were short and simple. Cody passed the test without any problems.

A couple of days later, they all gathered in the meeting room, and the district attorney explained to Cody that he would be going in front of the grand jury the following week and he would have to tell his stories once again. This time, the district attorney would be indicting the right people, and Cody would have to put himself right in the middle and tell everyone he was there in the mix of everything. He had to hold up his part and follow everything through to the end.

Cody assured them he would and told him not to forget that he wanted his freedom when it was all over. The district attorney leaned toward Cody and told him not to worry. "That will be in the bag, but I need convictions on Ramon and the whole group."

Trooper Chase stepped in again and said, "I'm sure he will do fine."

They took Cody and placed him into a minimum security prison. He had to be in twenty-four-hour lockup. They hid him away from all of the other inmates so nobody knew he was there. They changed his name as an added protection. Any guards that might have guessed Cody was there had great respect for him for what he did saving all their fellow officers' lives. The guards union was on his side as well.

The following week, Cody went in front of the grand jury.

He answered every question the district attorney had asked, right to the smallest detail. Cody told the grand jury about each and every murder and every person's involvement, including his own role. After he was through, some of the people on the jury were in shock from what Cody and his murderous associates had done in the prison.

The district attorney asked Cody one last question. "Did anyone offer you any deals or promises for your testimony?"

Cody stated yes and then explained what the terms were and explained his attorney had everything in writing. The district attorney wanted everyone in the grand jury to understand that he had to deal with the devil to get everyone else in hell. That was how he put it. He was being honest.

The grand jury brought down all the murder incitements once again that day. They brought each group of three inmates in one at a time for their court hearings. This time, Ramon, Duke, and all the other guys knew the district attorney's office had someone on the inside. It didn't take long for them to find out it was Cody. Based on Cody's advice, Trooper Chase suggested the prison officials keep each and every one of them separated from each other by placing them all in different prisons and keeping them apart from one another.

Cody knew if they had no communication with each other it would make it harder for them to find anything out, plan anything against him, or come up with a plan on how to beat the charges. He knew he had to stay one step in front of everybody. His life was on the line, and he had a great shot of walking out of prison a free man. He wasn't going to let anything or anybody get in his way.

The district attorney took a lot of heat for bringing more indictments down and costing the taxpayers of Massachusetts more money for the upcoming trials, but he stepped up in front of the news cameras and guaranteed convictions. Cody had to stay in total lockup and was bounced from prison to prison and jail to jail. He stayed in touch with Trooper Chase by phone three times a day. Cody knew it sucked, but he looked at it as an investment to be free. It took about fourteen months for the first trial to start, and Ramon and his crew were the first up at bat.

Chase picked Cody up from the prison a few days before the trial started. They set him up in a nice hotel and got him anything he needed. Chase even sent a whore up to his room to sleep with him every night. "Don't tell my boss about this or we both will be in big trouble," he told Cody.

Cody laughed. "Is this what you do with all the other informants?"

"Hell no," Chase said. "I told you, Cody, I'm going to take care you, and I haven't let you down yet, right?"

Cody agreed, and Chase lit up a joint and asked Cody if he remembered the last time they smoked.

"Hell yes," Cody said. "I thought you were going to have a heart attack when I banged on your police cruiser that night." They both laughed.

The day of the trial came and Cody was very nervous. Trooper Chase reminded Cody what to do. "Don't lie. Just tell the truth and look straight into the eyes of the person asking you the question. Don't look at Ramon and the boys. They are going to try to stare you down. Don't be intimidated and don't go off at the attorneys. You know they are going to try and get you to snap." Chase told Cody he would be sitting in the back of the courtroom and to look at him if he started getting nervous.

"Don't worry. I've been on that side many times, and I'll stay calm" Cody said.

When Cody was called to take the stand, he took the oath and glanced over at Ramon. Ramon was trying to get Cody to lock eyes with him, but Cody caught himself. He started looking all over the courtroom, looking for Chase but couldn't find him. He felt very nervous and uncomfortable. He knew he had to get control of himself and regain his composure.

The Assistant District Attorney, Donna Stevens stood up and started asking Cody some questions. Cody started to relax, looked into her eyes, and felt better. Ramon and the other two guys' attorneys tried to rip Cody's testimony apart, but Cody didn't let them get inside his head.

Their attorneys even went as far as to ask Cody where he was living and what deal he'd made for the lies he was telling. Cody told them he had been locked up twenty-four hours a day and was still in a prison. Cody also admitted to not only being involved in the murders, but helping plan each and every murder along with all three of the inmates sitting across from him. The courtroom got quiet after his statement. Cody felt he had closed the case.

Cody held his ground and didn't let them get to him. He spoke very convincingly to the jury. He lasted on the stand for two days straight and kept his head held high. The jury went out to deliberate, and it took them a day and a half to come back in with a verdict.

Everyone was on edge. Cody observed what the other side looked like while waiting for a jury to come in with a verdict. He waited under guard in the court office to hear something, and he was feeling out of sorts. Then Trooper Chase, the district attorney, and his assistant entered the room.

The district attorney slammed his papers on the desk and looked at Cody right in the eye. "You son of a bitch," he said.

Cody started to panic. "What happened?" he asked, thinking they had been found not guilty.

"I could kiss you right now," the D.A. smiled and said. "We did it. First degree murder on all three." He was really excited and hugged Cody.

Trooper Chase smiled and said the next trial would start next month. "Just do what you did at this trial and you'll be home free soon."

The district attorney agreed. "You will be a free man soon after we get them all."

Cody had to go back into lockup again until the next trial. He read the papers the next day. They pictured the district attorney gloating, with his hand held high and his index finger pointed. He was quoted as stating, "This is a victory for everyone who works in the prisons and justice system, and we will stop all these murder in the prison system." Cody knew he was making speeches for his future. The people of his county and the state of Massachusetts started to like this guy and how he stood for justice.

A reporter asked him if he would think about running for attorney general in Massachusetts, and the district attorney had turned to walk away, but then stopped and told the reporter, "I believe I could do more for this state if I worked in Washington." Cody knew that was the bait. He was feeding the voters and setting himself up down the road. Trooper Chase knew he was shooting for Washington and that he would take nothing less. Cody knew Chase would help him get there.

Cody showed up for each and every one of the trials and testified without any problems. They seemed to get easier for him. Everyone indicted was found guilty of first degree murder and received a life sentences with no chance of a parole. They also gave a plea bargain to Tony from the plate shop. He ended up with ten to fifteen years in the same prison in which he used to work for drug trafficking and bringing the bullets into the prison. He got off lucky. They had originally planned to charge him with conspiracy to commit murder for bringing in the bad dope that had helped kill people.

After all was said and done, the prison medic also pleaded guilty and received two years in a house of correction, and fifty-five guards all lost their jobs and never had any shot of working in any law enforcement position ever again. The prison had new rules and better training for the guards. New guidelines were implemented and all for the better. Cody really did hope that other younger kids like his friend Sean would be saved from being murdered.

The superintendent became the commissioner of correction, and his deputy took over his spot as superintendent. Under

Cody's advice, they formed special units and posted more guards to monitor each and every movement of the inmates.

Cody started working as an informant and four long years passed. The murder rate in the maximum security prison dropped 98 percent because of the special training correctional officers received through federal grants and the guards union. Through the advice of the state police, a new prison staff, and Cody, it all turned around for the better.

Chapter Thirty-Three

Now that the district attorney had everything he wanted, Cody wanted his freedom. They followed through with their part, and Cody received a hearing date to see the parole board. It was scheduled two months down the road, and Cody was happy about it. He hoped everything would go smooth the day he went in for his hearing.

Cody's day came, and he went in for his hearing to see the parole board in Boston. The full board was made up of seven members that had been appointed by the governor of the state. They asked Cody extensive questions about the crime for which he was first sent to prison. They then asked Cody about his prison records and his escapes. After Cody made a short statement, he sat down.

"This is a joke, right?" one board member said to Cody.

Cody asked Mr. Chambers, the head of the parole board, "What are you talking about? I signed an agreement with the district attorney's office."

"Well let's start with what you accomplished while you have been in prison," he said. "You have two escapes, several murders you've admitted to participating in. You have a sociopathic personality, and I don't have all day to go down the list of your whole prison record. You tell me, Cody, what do you expect from this board today? You think we are going to let you run free on the streets? Because, I think if we let you out, you'll end up killing another twenty people who look at you the wrong way just over the first weekend."

Cody's heart raced, and he didn't know what to say. He

quickly looked over at Trooper Chase for some help. He knew this guy was right. The only reason Cody was there in front of the board was because a deal had been made on his behalf.

Trooper Chase and some prison officials spoke on Cody's behalf, explaining to the board that if he hadn't been involved with those groups, they would have never gotten any convictions. They told the board how Cody saved many officials' lives and how he was a great asset to the state police and the district attorney's office.

Another board member asked Trooper Chase, "How can you be sure this inmate will not go out on the streets again and kill somebody else? He has a bad temper. He has proven he can kill and hurt people at any given time. How do know for sure we're not letting a walking time bomb back out into society?"

"Yes," another board member stated. "I would like to know the answer to that question, and I noticed here from the prison paperwork that he was seen by the prison psychologist fifteen years ago, and the doctor clearly stated he felt Cody had a sociopathic personality and could act out on any murder by forefeeling his enjoyment at any time. And after reading his prison records, the doctor was right on the money many years ago."

The same board member asked if Cody had received an updated evaluation by other professionals regarding his mental condition other than his diagnosis fifteen years ago. Cody really started to panic and wondered where they were going with this shit. He had thought it was all set, that he would walk in, get asked a few questions, and leave with a date for his release. *Something is wrong here*, he said to himself.

Trooper Chase started getting annoyed. "Look, I've worked for the state police for over twenty years, and I have never come before a parole board asking for any inmate to be released. You have a letter from the district attorney's office requesting a pardon for Cody, and you have prison officials telling you how many lives he saved from a takeover of a prison which would resulted in mass murder if it wasn't for this person coming forward, and I am requesting you release him back into society."

Another board member stated very clearly for the record, "We understand what went on behind closed doors with the deals that were made, Trooper Chase, and we will take everything into consideration of what Cody did for the prison and the district attorney's office, but put yourself in our position. This inmate and his past history show us he will never change, and some citizen out on the streets might make him angry. What action will he take?

"He was released into the prison population and other inmates feared this one man standing before us, and murders happened under his direction. I also have to add, he spent many years in the prison's segregation unit locked up twenty-three hours a day. If prison society couldn't control Cody, how can we trust him in our society?"

Trooper Chase jumped up and fired back, "Look, if you keep him in the system, we can't guarantee his safety. If you keep him in prison, it will only be a matter of time before he will end up dead or other people will die. Is this board going to keep him in prison to die and have his death on your hands? Your and everyone else's job on this parole board is to help an inmate out by releasing them back into society. If you choose not to parole Cody, you're acting like a judge, jury, and executioner today, and I want that on record for my own reasons."

It got very quiet. The head board member called for a five minute break. After five minutes, they all returned to the hearing and asked if anyone had anything to add.

Trooper chase stood up one last time. "I will assure you Cody will be fine if given a chance for parole," he stated.

With that, they told Cody he would get their answer within two weeks and thanked them all for coming.

Cody and Chase talked outside the room.

"What the fuck happened in there, Mark?" Cody asked. "I

thought this would be all set. I was hoping to come here and get a date by next week and be free.

"I'll make some calls," Chase said. "Go back and sit tight. I'll be in touch."

Trooper Chase called his boss, told him what happened at the board, and told him he had to follow through with his deal and make some calls, and he did. The D.A. made a call to someone in the governor's office and they ordered the board chairman to convince the other members to make it happen and not to ask any questions.

Chapter Thirty-Four

Cody went back into lockup once again, thinking he was going to get fucked over in some way. He felt something was not right. A week went by, and Chase came in to see him. He told Cody him the board had given him a date.

"Hell yes, that's great!" Cody yelled.

"Calm down," Chase said. "There are a couple of stipulations the board wanted that I agreed to."

The first thing was that they wanted Cody to have a full psychological evaluation by an institute on the street, not by the prison doctors. Chase said the evaluation should only take a day. The other stipulation was that they wanted him to serve six months in a pre-release center to prove he could work and hold a job and to give him time to get his head together and prepare him to be back in society. They would then parole him for the rest of his life.

"How I am going to be alright at a pre-release?" Cody asked. "Everyone knows who I am, and everyone who ever went through prison in the past fifteen years knows what I'm about."

Trooper Chase tried to explain to him that the times had changed out in the streets. "You've been locked up a long fucking time, well over fifteen years, and your head will be a little messed up just walking out there with no structure at all." He then reminded Cody that he had nothing out here at all. "You have to start fresh. Do you think you could just walk out of here like your partner Johnny did? Your partner was set up to fail when he was released from prison."

He told to Cody he thought the parole board was right in

everything they had to say. "You do have some issues going on in your head, and when you go back out in those streets, you're going to realize how right everyone was. And remember, Cody, don't act on your anger. Stop hurting people because your feelings are hurt. This is your only shot in life. There's only death after this."

"I understood all too well about death," Cody said. "It has been my best friend all my life."

"Six months will not be long," Chase said. "Hell, you just banged out over fifteen years. This should be a walk in the park for you. You'll be on the streets every day and start your life over again. All you will be doing there is sleeping. You can go do what you want on the weekends."

Cody thought about it and agreed, but he knew he had no choice. He was a little worried about getting the psychological evaluation. Chase told him he was worried about that, too. "But let's see what happens and be grateful the Department of Correction isn't doing the evaluation or they would have you in a straight jacket after the doctors were finished with you." They laughed.

The following week, Cody was released to the pre-release center. Trooper Chase and the new commissioner had him placed in a small pre-release center out in the woods in the western part of the state. It only held about fifteen inmates, none of which had even seen a real prison. All of those guys were from the local county jails. Cody had a new name and everybody there worked and did their own things. Cody was very excited about getting out, and he didn't know anyone in that place. He took a job cleaning cars for a car dealership.

Cody also went down to see a shrink for his evaluation. When he got there, they had him take several writing tests. Cody found the tests very hard. He thought they were all trick questions because all of the answers were kind of the same. Cody only could check off one answer. They then hooked wires to his head and laid him on a comfortable table for two hours. He fell asleep.

He didn't understand any of it and tried not to let it bother him. Some of the questions they asked him were way out in left field like, "Do you hate your mother? Did you ever run down the street naked or did you ever kill any animal? Did you ever kill your pets or ever hurt a dog or a cat?"

He answered no to all of their silly questions, but then remembered a time when he was about eleven years old. Cody and a couple of his buddies grabbed this beagle hound dog that used to bark and howl all the damn time. It had been quite annoying.

His two buddies hung a rope over a tree and hung the dog by its collar, and Cody took a hockey stick and whacked it across the chest. They left it hanging on the tree. As Cody ran back to his house, he could hear the dog still howling. Cody made it back to his house, went to bed, and hurting that dog bothered the shit out of him. He wondered if his friends went back and killed it.

The next day, he hooked up with his buddies, and they told him they killed the dog. They asked Cody to run down his friend's cellar and grab a shovel so they could bury it. Cody felt sad for the dog, and as he went through the door, they closed it behind and locked him in. Cody banged on the door, yelling for them to open it and let him out. They stood on the other side laughing the whole time. The cellar was dark, and Cody couldn't see much. He heard a noise.

He found the light and pulled the string. When the light came on, the beagle dog they said was dead started howling and barking at him. His buddies thought it would be funny to chain it up and lock Cody up in the cellar with the mutt to scare him, and it did. Cody remembered how he almost shit himself when he saw that dog in the cellar, thinking it was dead. Then Cody walked over to the pooch. The dog wagged its tail and licked Cody's face as he gave it a big hug and told the dog how sorry he was for hitting it. From that time on, he never hurt another animal ever again.

Cody finished his testing and called Chase and asked him to get the results before the board did so they knew were they stood. Chase agreed, and they received the results the following week. The board cleared Cody without any mental problems at all. Trooper Chase laughed and told Cody the results couldn't be right and wanted to know how a certified sociopath beat the test. Cody cracked up and said he didn't understand it either.

"I can't wait to tell the guys back at the office about this one," Trooper Chase told Cody. "Now I'm convinced these entire tests they give people are all a big joke, and it's all about the money."

Chapter Thirty-Five

Chase started to pick Cody up some weekends, and they went back to Chase's house and smoked pot and drank plenty of beer. He kept at least two ounces of pot in his freezer all the times, and had his wife cook steaks on the grill. Cody knew it was wise to keep Chase in his back pocket just in case he needed him to get him out of any shit. He still worked as a state trooper for the district attorney's office, but Cody knew he was going to retire in another year and move on to something else.

Cody was released from the pre-release center with life parole. He had to call into his parole officer once a month. The guy never had a problem with him because he knew Cody was hanging with Trooper Chase. Cody moved into his own place, and found himself wishing he had tucked away some of the money he had made in prison. He took a job working in a kitchen as a cook. He met a girl there and hooked up with her. Soon they moved in together, and he got along great with her. She knew he had just been released from the prison system but knew very little about him as a person. They hit it off right from the start and took it one day at a time.

She was the only person other than Chase who knew he had been in prison for murdering a guy sixteen years ago. She had a lot of questions to ask Cody, but she chose not to. She came from a respected family in a small suburban town, and they never had any idea at all about Cody, except for her father. He knew Cody was different than most people from the way he acted.

Cody soon realized he did have a problem adjusting to the streets. When he drove down the highway, he started having panics attacks, and when he was in large crowds, his heart would start palpitating. He was a man who had controlled everything all his life, but he didn't understand what was happening within his mind. It was all new to him. He wasn't in his eight-by-twelve cell or protected by a thirty-foot wall when he went out for a walk.

Cody was out in the open, and everyone around him didn't know anything about what he had been through. Cody knew he could never tell anyone. People at his work already felt uncomfortable being around him at certain times. Cody knew people on the streets had their own problems, worked hard to pay whatever bills they had, and supported their families. It was new to him. He'd never even held a real job before. When he wanted money, Cody had just taken it.

Cody slowly started to understand that everything had changed over the years, and it was going to take time for him to adjust. He remembered the times he'd escaped from prison. He'd really had no real reason to escape other than not wanting to go along with the system. There had been nothing for him out on the streets back then. He just escaped just to see if he could do it. He knew he was going to get caught if he stayed around in Boston. He now understood why all the other inmates hadn't taken off and tried to escape.

For his whole life, Cody had always tried to stay ahead of the game and other people. He knew he had to stay away from trouble. He knew he could never go back to prison. It would be a sure death for him. Cody promised himself that if the time came for the cops to ever take him back ever again, he would go out in a blaze of glory and take a few of them with him. He started to realize the real world shit was not easy and understood more about why inmates returned to prison.

Cody knew he had to try control his anger and made a commitment to himself that if he had to kill someone, he would take a step back and think things out before taking any immediate action. Cody drove into the woods and down dirt roads and found a couple of places to dig graves for safe keeping, just in case he had to put some bodies in them. He knew if the time came to use them, he would be all set.

He had to cover all his tracks. With the way his mind worked, Cody even thought about cutting the bodies up and running the parts through a wood chipper if he had too. But he hoped he wouldn't have to.

He had one thing in his favor when it came to pulling a crime or taking someone out. He was never afraid to work alone. As a kid, he'd always had Johnny to call on if he needed him. But by working alone, he only had himself to blame if he ever got caught. Cody now was a free man and every cop's nightmare if he chose it to be. He had more experience in crime than twenty-year cops working the streets anywhere in the country. He'd had plenty of time to learn from the best, and from not only his mistakes in life, but everyone else's, too.

He knew back in the day, if guys were going to rob a bank or make a hit on somebody, some of them would dress up like a women to pull it off. He knew it really worked. When his friends did it, all the witnesses only remembered seeing a woman run away. And the cops then looked for a women running down the street. His friends would duck into a doorway, change quickly, and walk down the street watching the cops drive right by.

Cody understood that most people pulled a crime or killed a person with other people and then wondered why they got caught. They didn't realize the cops just needed to catch one person and that person would sell everybody out for lesser or no time. Or some would go and brag about what they did and get themselves caught that way.

Out of everything Cody knew in his life, he understood how cops and the court systems worked. They got about 90 percent of all their arrests from informants and the other 10 percent was just luck or something they happened upon. Hell, that was how Cody had beat the system himself. Everyone in prison thought he was there to die, and he proved them all wrong because he was smarter than they were. Most of them were now dead or would die in prison, and he was a free man.

Cody would try to stay clean and not look for any trouble with the cops or his parole officer. He only worried about running into someone from the past or how he would react if someone gave him a hard time. He had a plan in effect for any future problems. He also knew he had to get some help, so he started to see a doctor and got on medication to help relax him and get his mind straight.

Cody couldn't believe how messed up his head was and remembered when they released his partner Johnny. He thought about how his mind must have been. He knew Johnny would have had a gun on him back in the early days and blown that other guy away. But the system set him up to die when he was released.

Cody tried to go to counseling, but it had no effect. What was he going to tell some guy in a chair about his past and what he went through? He tried, and the guy felt uncomfortable listening to him. That's when Cody knew nobody on the streets would ever understand. It was like taking a war veteran from Vietnam who had been on the battlefield for years and then placing him back in the states and telling don't hurt anyone and go live a normal life. Yeah right.

Cody talked to Mark Chase about everything over the years, and Chase tried to keep Cody calm and relaxed. He tried to get Cody to understand how real life worked on the streets and how everything had changed. That's when Cody realized while time might change, people don't. People out there in the streets were the same assholes he knew back in the days.

He ended up moving into a small town in Massachusetts with his girl and everything went great for the first six months until one Saturday night around 11:30 PM. He was on his way home from work and accidently cut another car off when he pulled onto a main street. Cody was only two blocks from his home and thought nothing about it. Then he looked in the mirror and the other person was following him, flashing his lights on and off.

Cody turned up his street and pulled into his driveway, and the guy pulled in behind him, jumped out of his car, and ran toward Cody, making a scene and getting close to him. Cody reacted and punched the guy in the throat as hard as he could. The guy dropped to his knees and tried to catch his breath.

Cody helped stand the guy up and walked him back to his car, looking around to see if anyone noticed what happened. The guy was still holding his throat and trying to catch a full breath. Cody started to panic and thought the guy was going to call the cops. He knew he could never allow that to happen.

Cody talked to the guy and then said, "Let me see if you're alright."

The man lowered his hands and took a really deep breath. At that moment, Cody chopped him in the throat again even harder and the guy passed out, leaning over to his right side. Cody climbed on top of the guy to get his arm around his neck and strangled him until he was dead. It was over in less than a minute. Cody checked the man's pulse just to make sure he was really dead.

Cody pushed the body to the floor of the passenger side of the guy's car and ran into his garage to grab a shovel, a screwdriver, and a flash light. He tossed everything in the back seat and drove guy's car to one of the unmarked graves he had dug previously.

Cody swore all the way to the grave site, yelling at the bastard he had just killed, telling the dead guy, "You had to be a fucking tough guy, didn't you? Look at the problem you just caused me."

He finally arrived at the unmarked grave site, pulled the body out of the car, and then jammed the screwdriver deep into the man's right ear. Cody then turned the guy's head and jammed it into his other ear, penetrating his brain once again. He wanted to make sure that the guy was dead. He tossed the body into the open grave, shoveled dirt over it, and kicked some dead leaves around to cover the grave marker. He hid the shovel, knowing he would return in the daylight to make sure everything checked out okay.

Cody drove the dead guy's car to the parking lot of a store that was open twenty-four hours a day and wiped everything down so he didn't leave any fingerprints behind. He walked back to his home, which was only a mile away. He took a shower, had a few drinks, and thought about what had just happened. He couldn't understand why the guy had come after him.

Cody wasn't mad. As a matter of fact, he felt great. It was the best he had felt in a long time. The altercation had been over in no time. He dealt with the situation and solved the problem his way. He took another sip of his drink and smiled, realizing that this was all he needed to do to feel good again. It was better than taking the medication the doctor gave him.

Cody's girlfriend woke up and came downstairs. "Are you alright, babe? I heard you talking to someone."

"No, I'm fine," Cody said. "I was just talking out loud."

"How was work tonight?" she asked.

Cody smiled and took her into his arms. He looked into her eyes, told her it was the best night he had in a very long time, and took her to bed.

Cody woke up the next morning and drove down to the grave site. He covered up things a little more discreetly. He wanted to make sure no one would stumble across the grave in the future. He threw his shovel in the trunk, drove home, and washed it off.

A few days later, he read in the local paper that a man was missing and they had found his car with the keys in it. Cody smiled, thinking it had been way too easy. Suddenly the phone rang, breaking Cody's concentration.

It was Chase. He asked Cody if he wanted to get together and hang out.

"Sure," Cody replied. "I have nothing planned. Let me get cleaned up and I will be over soon." When Cody arrived, they started bullshitting. They always had a blast because they both understood and felt each other's pain.

While Cody and the guys back in the joint had been killing people, Chase had been the homicide cop that came in to figure out what happened and clean up the mess. Chase had dealt with his share of murders on the streets and in the prisons. Over time, it all had messed with Chase's head as well. He told Cody about the time he saw five little babies out in the woods with their throats slashed by their own parents and old ladies and mothers who had been killed for purses that only had five dollars them.

It had taken its toll on the both of them, but that was the difference between Cody and Chase. Chase not only had to see this shit after it happened, but he had to figure out how it happened and who did it. Cody understood why he got high most of the time. It was just like the inmates in the prison. He had to escape reality. But with Cody, it was different. Cody felt better after hurting someone. Not in the sense of torture, but it let him release all of his frustrations. And he didn't have to be high either. The one thing about killing someone or pulling an armed robbery was that criminals got hooked on it like drugs. It was so addicting that they just wanted more and more.

Chase soon threw in his towel for retirement. He said he'd had enough of being a cop. Cody asked him what he was going to do. He laughed at Cody and told him maybe he'd take over the Department of Corrections and become the new commissioner or grab some chief of police job in some small town. Cody knew Chase had the connections to get any job he wanted within the state. He was still young enough and always said retirement would just kill him at an early age if he didn't do something.

Cody realized he needed something in his life to keep him on the right track. He was always worried about getting close to someone and caring for a special person. In the past, the people he cared about had always died or gotten him into trouble. He always thought about his little friend Sean and how he used to tell Cody about how he and his family had lived and done everything together. They had fun until his father turned into a drunk and ruined everything.

Cody thought about having his own family. He knew that he would never allow his kids to be without anything and he would always be there for them. Cody decided to take a chance and ask his girl to marry him. She did.

Chase laughed at Cody and told him he thought he was fucking nuts for getting married. "You think you had problems in your past fifteen years, wait till you have to live with a woman for the rest of your life."

Cody just shook his head and smiled, knowing that Chase still supported his decision. He agreed to be Cody's best man. After the wedding, Cody wanted to get away from Massachusetts for a while, so he took his new wife moved out of state. They wanted to start fresh and have a family. They ended up in New York, right near the Connecticut border. Chase was able to have Cody's parole transferred up there.

Soon Cody had a baby on the way, and it gave him great pleasure knowing that would be his new life. Cody figured a family would help stabilize him and keep him out of shit. They moved to a neighborhood that was nothing but a headache from the start. People in New York just sucked. He realized why Bostonians hated New Yorkers. They were arrogant pricks. All they thought about was baseball, and they hated him immediately because of his accent.

Cody's wife was pregnant, and he had an asshole neighbor that busted everyone's balls. He played music all night long and pissed outside in the driveway. He was a neighborhood bully that did whatever he wanted.

Cody stopped him one day and asked him what his problem was and why he made everybody's lives so miserable.

"Fuck off or I'll beat the shit out of you," the guy said. He got in Cody's face. "Do you understand where I am coming from?"

Cody lowered his face so he didn't make eye contact and

told the guy, "Sure, I understand perfectly." He acted like he was intimidated and quickly walked away.

He knew the guy had to go because he wasn't going to put up with that prick. Cody's wife worked days, and he worked the night shift as a cook. He took a week off and followed the guy. He wanted to get a better understanding of what he did and what he was all about. The guy drove a trash truck by himself. He picked up Dumpsters behind stores early in the morning and had a steady route.

So Cody decided to stake out one location in particular and see what time the guy showed up to empty the Dumpster. He noticed he picked up the trash every other day around the same time. It was a busy store, and people were going in an out early in the morning getting their morning coffee. The Dumpster was located out in the back, and all the guy did was lower the two forks, drive in front of the Dumpster and lift it up over the truck. After the Dumpster was empty, he lowered it to the ground and moved on to the next stop on his route. Cody knew the truck was loud and that no one paid attention to a trash truck.

One morning, he parked his car over on the side of the store where the employees parked, only twenty yards away from the Dumpster. The guy pulled up in his trash truck, and Cody walked toward the cab of the truck. As the truck started to lift the Dumpster over its bed, Cody grabbed the side mirror with his left gloved hand and jumped up on the driver's side. He aimed his .22 caliber pistol at the guy's head, and before the asshole could even turn his head, *bang*—one shot. Cody aimed right under his left ear, knowing the bullet would penetrate the back of his brain.

Then Cody jumped off the truck and tossed the gun over into a wooded area located behind the store. He then casually walked back to his car, got in, and drove home. Cody was tired of these people giving him shit. He knew what the consequence would be if he got caught, but he knew he could do this all the time if he wanted to. After all, it was what he loved to do, and he knew all the tricks of the trade.

It was far too easy for Cody because he didn't know any of the people he was killing. As a matter of fact, it worked to his advantage. When the cops investigated a murder, they always looked at the family and friends first, and then they looked at who the deceased had problems with, where he hung out, and all that shit. Cody was sure nobody would ever miss him. The guy was a bully and a prick and needed to die.

Later that night as Cody and his wife ate dinner, she notice the cops outside and in the guy's house. She wanted to go over and see what was going on, but Cody told her outright, "Honey, I have one rule in life: if it don't concern you then don't get involved." He then said, "Now let's finish supper and get on with our night."

Time went by and they had their first child and named it after Cody. Cody had kept in touch with Chase and found out the district attorney he'd helped out had moved on to Washington. He was elected into the House. A week after that, Chase retired from the Massachusetts state police.

Four months went by, and Chase called Cody up and told him he had a new job. "You're never going to believe what it is," Chase said and then told him the governor had appointed him head of the Massachusetts Parole Board.

"Get the hell out of here," Cody said. "You're messing with me!"

"Nope," Chase said. "I was approved by his counsel last week and was sworn into office today. I just got home and I didn't want to tell you until it was official. I am starting my new job next week."

"That's great," Cody told him.

"Do you know what this means?" Chase asked.

"What," Cody said.

"That means we can get you off your life parole," Chase said.

"Oh my God, I didn't even think of that," Cody said.

Chase told him to give him six months to a year because it would give him time to understand how the parole system worked.

"No problem," Cody said.

While waiting almost a year, Cody stayed cool and kept a low profile. By that time, he and his wife had another child and got tired of living up in New York, so they took their two kids back to Massachusetts. Good old Mark Chase was happy to see Cody back, and they kept in touch every couple of weeks.

Of course, Chase asked Cody how he made out up in New York and if he had run into any problems.

Cody smiled and told him, "You know how those New Yorkers are, Chase. They are so predictable, and you always have to deal with each of them on an individual basis."

Cody asked Chase about having his life parole removed.

"I'm way ahead of you buddy," Chase said. "Your parole will be gone in another three months, and I'm also having your record expunged."

Cody couldn't believe it. He could not believe Chase was doing that for him. He shook Chase's hand vigorously and thanked him profusely.

"You will be the first lifer in this state to ever have life parole removed," Chase then told him.

"My God, I'm impressed," Cody said with excitement.

"See Cody, I told you I would take care of you. You did right by me and I will do right by you. Now, many years later, I have kept my word to you and I never let you down, did I?"

"No you didn't let me down, my friend. You definitely didn't let me down," Cody said.

Cody went home and told his wife the great news. He said now there was nothing holding him back and he had to answer to no one. Cody had started his family and he had his one friend, Mark Chase. He worked every day and tried hard and not get into stealing shit or hurting any more people. He did have some small problems with bosses he worked for and people that gave him shit on the streets.

It was hard for him each day to keep his mouth shut and do nothing, but the balance of having a family kept his thought process in line. But in the back of his mind, there was always Plan B. He always knew where he could find an extra grave somewhere if he needed to unload some stress. His wife and Chase would never know.

Since he was released from prison, Cody had been keeping a list in the back of his mind of everyone that gave him or his family a hard time. He would someday get them back on his time. He kept that mental list and swore that if a doctor ever gave him six months to live or something ever happened to his family, he would kill every last fucking one of them. He would commit the biggest mass murder streak the country had ever seen. He laughed about his idea in his own head because no one knew his plan.

Cody still sat around with Chase sometimes on weekends and listened about who was coming up for parole, who Chase was letting out, and who he was going to keep in. Sometimes Chase even asked Cody for his opinion about certain guys he thought would be a good candidate to be let out on the streets. Cody would laugh and tell Chase to let the entire prison out. Who gave a fuck? If they let him out, everyone should be able to get out.

As time passed, Cody grew older. He'd never had a problem escaping prisons, but he realized that he could never escape his past. It ate at him each and every day of his life. He still missed his friends. But because most of them were dead, he realized he was not afraid of dying anymore. Death seemed to have worn Cody out over the years. He and death were still the best of friends. All he could hope for was that when he died, if there was another life, he hoped to run into his friends Johnny and Sean.

Mark Chase and Cody still smoke their pot and drank their beer. To this very day when Cody gets quiet, Chase asks him what he is thinking about. Cody always puts on that smile of his, looks over at his old friend, and just shakes his head, Chase smiles back and understands that Cody has made it.

They fish together on the weekends when they can and reminisce about the good old days. It is all either of them have to hang on to—the past. They rely on and counsel each other, talking about everything that has happened to each of them over the years. They also know and understand that they need each other.

They both came from the same neighborhood and went in different directions to survive over the years. Now they both now live by an old saying of General MacArthur: "Old soldiers never 'die' they just fade away."